Don't Call Me Marda

Author/Illustrator Sheila Kelly Welch

Don't Call Me Marda

Our Child Press
Wayne, Pennsylvania

J
Welch

Text and illustrations copyright © 1990 by Sheila Kelly Welch

Our Child Press
800 Maple Glen Lane
Wayne, PA 19087-4727

Manufactured in the United States of America
hardcover: ISBN 09611872-3-9
paperback: ISBN 09611872-4-7

Library of Congress Cataloging-in-Publication Data

Welch, Sheila Kelly.
    Don't call me Marda.

    Summary: Marsha feels apprehensive about her parents' plans to adopt a retarded child.
    1. Mentally handicapped -- Fiction.   2. Adoption -- Fiction) I. Title.
PZ7.W44894Do   1990   (Fic)   89-92420
ISBN 0-9611872-3-9
ISBN 0-9611872-4-7 (pbk.)

For my mother
and
in memory of my father

TRICT

1

With her head resting against the school bus window, Marsha O'Dell could feel the vibration from the rough, potholed road. It hurt, but the window was pleasantly cool. Even though outside it was unusually warm for January, the heater in the bus was turned up full force.

Marsha shrugged inside her thick winter jacket, then glared at the driver's back. She knew better than to ask grouchy Ol' Cranstram to lower the heat. Instead, she unwrapped her long knitted scarf, lumped it into a ball, and propped it between her head and the window. Now sweat dampened her armpits, so she unzipped her jacket, then she shut her eyes.

"Wake up." It was Rosie's voice in a harsh whisper.

"I am awake." Marsha didn't open her eyes. She knew her best friend was sitting on the aisle side of the seat in front of her.

The two girls always started the ride home sitting together.

Then, as the bus emptied out on its long trip through the Pennsylvania countryside, they would separate, place their books on the empty seats, and enjoy the space.

Now there were only four passengers left on the bus. Rosie's nine-year-old sister, Lily, was sitting in front, so she could chat with Ol' Cranstram and listen to him grunt. At the back of the bus, slouching low in his seat, was Mike Adams. He always moved to that position when the last of the high school students got off the bus several stops earlier.

Marsha stared at the blank darkness behind her eyelids. There was something safe and calm about the empty world of her closed eyes.

If I were blind, she thought, I wouldn't know that Rosie has blue eyes and almost black hair, and she's so pretty the teenage boys are starting to stare at her. I wouldn't know what I look like either—mousey brown hair, grey eyes like a cloudy day. The best part would be that I wouldn't care. I didn't used to care.

"If you're awake, how come you're not answering me?" Rosie demanded.

"What?" Marsha opened her eyes and blinked. "I told you. I am awake."

Rosie snorted. "Yeah, well, I asked if you want me to come over tomorrow morning so we can play Barbies. I can't tonight. We've got two new calves, and I've got to feed them. Dad knows I can't resist their big brown eyes and cute, wiggly noses. It's all part of his plot to turn me into a farmer. He's given up on Violet. Ever since she started at the community college, he figures she's bound to move away for good."

"I know. You told me before. What about Ivy?"

"What about the little brat?" Rosie wrinkled her nose in distaste.

"Being a farmer."

"No way! She stepped in a cow pie the other day and got hysterical. Five years old and already her main ambition is to be Miss America. Lily's just as bad. Ask her to clean a stall and she breaks out in hives."

"You'd better not be talkin' about me!" shouted Lily. "You

heard what Mom said this morning."

"Poor Dad," Rosie whispered, cupping her hand around her mouth, pretending to tell Marsha a secret. Lily stuck out her tongue and turned back toward the driver.

"He always wanted a son," Rosie continued with an exaggerated sigh. " 'Course I don't know what my parents would've called a boy. Petunia, maybe? Or Crocus? Anyhow, maybe I will be a farmer."

Marsha nodded without enthusiasm. She was tired of hearing Rosie talk about the future. Sometimes her friend's ideas were sort of interesting, like the plan in which the two of them would raise horses on their jointly owned land. That appealed to Marsha. In general, though, Marsha didn't feel comfortable with any sort of change.

"You want me to come over, or what?" Rosie asked.

"Sure! If it stays warm, we'll play in the hayloft." Marsha bit one fingernail thoughtfully and said, "Rosie? You don't think we're getting too old to play Barbies, do you?"

"Play? Play Barbies?" Rosie shook her head. "We don't play! We create life dramas. It's good practice, you know. You like writing stories. Maybe someday we'll both be famous authors."

There she goes again, talking about growing up, Marsha thought as she turned toward the window. She used her scarf to wipe away the condensation, so she could watch the familiar landscape.

The bus lumbered uphill, and Ol' Cranstram braked for a curve. Marsha's books skidded off the seat. She scrambled after them, and when she sat up again and looked out, the trees were gone, replaced by frozen fields exposed to the weak winter sun.

The new housing development on the left side of the road looked barren and bleak. Fourteen houses had been built along a new, raw street that looped away from the main road and then back again. Somehow the contractor had miscalculated, and an early winter had left the development unoccupied because of septic system problems. Now the empty houses stared with blank windows at the dead field.

Mike Adams' house had been built first, almost two years

before. It was on the main road, but it looked as if it belonged to the development.

Marsha squinted at the ranch style houses, feeling again her resentment at their intrusion into her world. She'd always thought of that entire field as her own even though she knew her family's property line was near the base of the hill, at the edge of the woods.

For several years the field had not been planted with a crop, so wild grass grew there abundantly. Marsha had often ridden her pony, Butterscotch, across the creek, out of the woods, and up the long hill. The wind would push against her face as they galloped, sending her hair into a tangled frenzy.

When the construction had begun last summer, she'd gone back again and again to watch and fuel her anger at the destruction.

One afternoon a workman had yelled at her, "Get the hell away from here, kid! You'll get hurt!"

Hunched over with embarrassment, she rode Butterscotch home. It had rained the night before, and her sneakers were drenched from touching the tall, wet grass. She realized suddenly that she'd grown too big for her pony.

Since that day she hadn't gone back up the hill.

The bus lurched to a stop. Mike was already halfway up the aisle, almost next to Marsha.

"Shit!" he said loudly as he slammed against the corner of her seat.

"Watch the language, boy. I'll write you up," Cranstram growled as he glared in the rearview mirror.

Mike recovered and sauntered to the front of the bus. "Sorry, Mr. Cranstram," he said, exaggerating his polite tone. "I didn't mean to offend your sensitive ears."

"Off!" Cranstram barked.

"So long, Marsha Marshmallow. See you Monday, Bowwow Bower!" Mike called over his shoulder.

"Get lost, Mikey. And while you're gone, think of some new lines!" Rosie yelled as he hopped off the bus.

The two girls watched Mike cross the road. He turned as he

started up the driveway, then he waved. A broad grin brightened his face.

Rosie leaned over and began gathering her books. "Sure'll be nice when those houses start to sell," she said to Marsha. "Maybe there'll be some cute boys. Mike's such a dork. Sorry, no offense. I know you used to like him. But you have to admit, we sure do need some new kids around here."

"We'll be getting one new kid—maybe even before summer," Marsha said slowly.

"What?" Rosie's eyes grew wide with interest. "You mean the sister you're adopting? Have you heard something? Come on! Tell me." Without waiting for an answer, she babbled on. "I still think it'd be better to get a boy. You know, a real handsome one about thirteen or fourteen!"

Marsha couldn't help grinning. Rosie had been putting in her request for a teenage boy ever since she'd heard about the O'Dells' plan to adopt a child.

"Don't get hyper, Rosie! We don't know anything definite. But Mom keeps saying she's sure we'll hear soon."

"You're lucky to be able to pick a sister. I just got stuck with mine. Violet, the stuck-on-herself teenager. Lily and Ivy, the mini-monster babies."

"I heard that!" Lily shot back. "I'm really gonna tell Mom if you don't cut it out."

"See what I mean?" Rosie rolled her eyes.

"I won't get to pick a sister, silly. That's not how adoption works. Least, I don't think so."

"Well, it should! Otherwise you might get a real loser. Some kind of weirdo!" Rosie pretended to gag as she stuck her finger in her mouth.

"All I know is that she's going to be younger than me," said Marsha, "but not a baby. Probably about five or six. I just hope she likes Butterscotch, so she'll learn to ride him. Dad keeps hinting around about selling him just 'cause I'm too big for him."

"Five? Yuk! Well, even if your sister's as bad as Ivy or even Lily, you'll still have me for your best friend."

Lily looked back and glared.

"Thanks." Marsha smiled at Rosie.

In a few seconds they would reach their bus stop, the last one on the route. Marsha pressed her books against her body, then leaned toward the window. With the tip of her finger, she drew a happy face in the misty lower corner.

The bus stopped, and as she got up Marsha stared at her drawing. The smile was a little crooked and wobbly, making the expression more worried than happy.

2

Marsha licked grape jelly off the edges of a slice of toast, her typical Saturday morning breakfast.

"Why does Mom have to buy this generic purple goop?" she asked her father. "It's so runny, I can't keep it on my toast."

David O'Dell looked up from the newspaper. He was working on a crossword puzzle, and his expression was vague.

"I guess it's cheap," he answered after a moment's pause.

Marsha ate the rest of her breakfast in large bites. She looked at her father carefully. She had never really thought about his growing old, yet she could see his hair was thinning on top, and his forehead seemed to be getting higher. His mustache, however, was just as thick as ever and in need of a trimming. Right now he was nibbling at it absentmindedly with his lower teeth.

An old radio sat in the middle of the table like a mechanical centerpiece. Marsha thought about changing the station but knew her father was listening even while he searched his mind for some obscure word.

She felt comfortable sitting here, licking jelly off her fingers, her father not noticing.

Suddenly he looked up. "Did you hear that? It's going to hit fifty-five degrees!"

"Good! Rosie'll be here soon. We're going to play Barbies in the hayloft."

"Barbies?" Her father's eyes focused on Marsha's face. "Those obscene characters? Aren't you getting a little old? Or maybe I'm mixed up. Perhaps you're finally old enough."

"Oh, Daddy. Stop teasing."

" 'Daddy?' I seem to remember a young lady who maintained she was going to call me by my given name." Her father smiled.

"You're still teasing! And I meant it about your name. Rosie's sister Violet calls their parents John and Lynn. She says it makes parents realize their kids are people, too. I'm just not used to it yet."

"That's okay. I forgive you. And I know you're a person even though you call me Daddy."

"Good!" Marsha grinned at him.

"And you've got purple goop on your nose."

"Daddy! Do I really?"

"No, I'm just kidding. But I promise to quit. Did you put Butterscotch out in the pasture?"

"Yeah. He's probably stuck in the mud by now."

There was a resounding knock at the kitchen door. Marsha hopped up and grabbed her play jacket off the hook next to the door as she swung it open.

"Hi, Marsha. Morning, David," Rosie said cheerfully.

"Shh, not so loud. Mom, I mean, Kate's still sleeping." Marsha gathered up her bulky paper bag filled with Barbie dolls and accessories.

As they left David said, "Have fun, girls. And please shut the door. It's still winter."

Outside Rosie skipped across the dead lawn, then slowed to tiptoe around a sprawling puddle in the driveway. "I'll be glad when real winter weather comes back. You should see our barnyard. It's all wet and sloppy. Yukkie!"

Rosie opened the Dutch door of the old barn with one hand. In the other she clutched her battered doll case, a hand-me-down from Violet.

"Remember how we used to swing on this door?" Marsha asked, closing the bottom half of the door behind them.

"Yeah, we pretended it was our pony. That was before you got Butterscotch."

The girls entered the barn, which was cool and empty of animals. Just a faint horsey odor hung in the still air.

Shafts of speckled light filtered down through tiny holes in the roof far above. When Marsha was small, she had tried to grab the dust-filled, golden air. Now she could still remember the sense of wonder mixed with disappointment when her fingers had turned bright themselves and grasped nothing.

"Race you to the top!" Rosie said as she began scrambling up the ladder to the loft. "I won!" she called out moments later from the topmost bales.

"No fair," Marsha gasped. "My bag's heavier. Slowed me down. I almost slid through a crack between the bales."

"Just like Vi's Barbie doll! Only she was between the bales for 'bout a year," Rosie said as both girls began to unpack their paraphernalia from bag and case.

"Ta-da! Here she is!" Rosie announced pulling out an old Barbie doll.

"Oh, no! She's bald again. What'd you do with her wig?" asked Marsha.

"I didn't do anything with it. Probably Lily has it, or maybe Ivy. They're always messing with my stuff. Just hope Vi never sees her best Barbie looking like this."

"You never told her you'd lost her?"

"Nah. She'd have had a hissy fit. She really didn't play with her dolls anymore, you know, but she didn't want me to have them either. Least ways, not to lose them in some old barn." Rosie giggled. "Bet the mice had soft nests that year."

"Since you don't have a wig for her," Marsha said, "we'll have to make the story fit her appearance, right?"

"Sure. How about she's been in a car accident. The car caught fire, and her hair got all burnt off?"

"Okay," Marsha agreed. The idea sounded a little grim, but she was glad to have Rosie make a suggestion.

"Let's say Barbie had been married about six months before the accident. Her husband, Rob, saved her. But now she's so ugly and weird-looking, he's sort of tempted to go out with somebody else," Marsha began the story.

Rosie nodded as she picked up Marsha's newest, most glamorous doll. Long blond hair hung in ringlets down her back.

"What'd you name her?" Rosie asked.

"Laura. Like my Aunt Laura."

"Oh, yeah. The one who lives in New York and looks like a model? She's neat."

"Sort of, I guess. But she's always trying to tell my parents what to do. She thinks Dad's wasting his talents way out here in the sticks teaching school. She thinks she knows best just 'cause she's his big sister."

"Sounds like Vi," Rosie said. "Okay, let's get started." She placed the bald Barbie on a bale of hay and held the one named Laura in a standing position.

Marsha picked up her Ken doll, named Rob, by the waist and turned him to look at Laura, then away.

"Hi, there, Handsome," Rosie said in her best Laura voice. "Wouldn't you like to have a drink with me? I understand your poor wife had a terrible accident. So sad, I mean, you know. It's a dreadful shame for you, poor dear. You must be so lonely with her off in the hospital."

"I was lonely," Marsha/Rob answered. "She's out of the hospital now, and she's improving. With treatment she may return to normal. I love my wife. I can't have a drink with you—now, or ever!"

"Ah, come on, Lover Boy," Laura pleaded in a most seductive tone. "I need you. I guess . . . I guess I'm the one who's lonely. Please, just one teensy-weensy drink?"

"Hell, Laura. What do you want? Isn't there anyone else you can talk to?" Rob's voice was desperate.

"There is no one I can talk to. Honest!" Laura was right next to Rob now, and her arm was resting stiffly on his shoulder.

"Just leave me alone, Laura! I have to take Barbie back to the hospital for a scalp treatment today."

"Can't she go by herself?" Laura pouted. "I understand she's lost all her hair and has tiny holes all over her head. How gross! It must really turn you off."

"This is too much," Marsha said in her normal voice. "Let's make up a different story. How about if Barbie's a rock star, and she shaved off her hair to give herself a new image?"

"Well, okay, I guess," said Rosie. "It is starting to sound like a soap opera. We could call it *Barbie's Hope.*"

"Or *Hairless Hospital* or *Bald and Beautiful.* No! I know . . . *The Young and the Hairless,*" suggested Marsha.

Rosie laughed and crossed her eyes. "Radical! Come on, let's start a different story. I like the rock star idea."

"We could call her Bold Bald Barbie," said Marsha. "She's getting ready for her first concert with no hair."

"Good. This'll give me a chance to sing," Rosie said with a grin.

Over an hour slipped by during which B.B.B.'s singing career skyrocketed and then plummeted off the charts. The girls suddenly began to realize that they were getting chilly and hungry. So they collected all the dolls, counted to insure against loss, and climbed down from the loft.

A grey pigeon fluttered across the empty space above their heads. Then his feet clutched a beam, and he cooed softly. Marsha whistled at him, and he cocked his head to peer down at them.

"You want to see Butterscotch?" Marsha asked.

"Sure. I haven't petted the ol' nag since last fall."

They found the little pony in the pasture. His light-brown coat was caked with mud.

Marsha glared at him. "Look! He rolled. He's filthy. And I spent an hour brushing him last night. Ungrateful wretch."

Butterscotch lifted his head and gazed solemnly at the two girls.

"I was going to ride you today," Marsha told him. She

reached out and straightened his golden forelock. "But now, if I do, I'll end up looking like a mud pie."

Rosie giggled. *"He's* the one who'll look like a mud pie when you squash him flat."

"No, he's strong enough to carry me. But you're right. I am too big for him."

"Well, when you sell him, you'll have money to buy a bigger horse, right?"

"You sound like my dad. He says it'd be better for Butterscotch to be with kids who'd ride him and exercise him. Says otherwise, we'll have to change his name to Butterball. But I have a plan all worked out," said Marsha slowly. "If my new sister learns to ride Butterscotch, we're bound to keep him." She glanced at Rosie. "Don't give me that bug-eyed look. We haven't heard a thing about her. Not a word. Gads! You're more excited about this whole deal than I am."

"Life can get dreadfully boring," Rosie said melodramatically.

Marsha ignored her. She whistled, and Butterscotch pricked his ears and looked at her with interest. She smiled, reliving again the rush of joy and love she'd felt the first time she'd ever seen him. It had been on her sixth birthday—her very own pony!

Marsha held out her arms. "See, Butter Boy? No bridle. None hidden in this old paper bag. Of course, you might like to nibble the hair off some of these dolls."

"Come on," Rosie said, glancing at her watch. "I'd better get home. It's almost lunchtime."

"Maybe you can eat with us. Let's go call your mom."

Butterscotch snorted, then tossed his head and ambled away.

Marsha watched him for a moment before grabbing her bag and following Rosie back to the house.

3

The wind moaned sadly beyond the windows of the old brick farmhouse. It was a familiar sound to Marsha, but tonight it made her feel particularly lonely.

She sat cross-legged on her bottom bunk and looked around her bedroom. Her gaze wandered over her shelves crammed with her favorite books, games, and her model horse collection. The horse shelf was much too small. If the poor animals ever came alive, she thought, they'd die of starvation with so little pasture land. On the wall above her shelves were magazine clippings—photographs of rock stars and race horses—attached with jagged hunks of masking tape.

There were several framed sketches which her father had drawn when he was younger—one of Marsha asleep in her crib and another of a flying horse. She wished that she had inherited his artistic talent. Although now he didn't do much art work, there had been a time when he'd considered becoming a commercial artist.

Building and painting Marsha's bed when she was four years old had been David's most recent artistic endeavor. Marsha still loved her bed, which was more like two boxes. Her father had painted woodland animals on the sides of the top and bottom bunks.

Marsha frowned now as she stared at the heap of dirty clothes on the floor and the scraps of paper, cat hairs, and lint adorning her blue rug. Everything about the room was familiar and comfortable. Yet, tonight her life had changed.

Getting up slowly, she went to her chest of drawers and began rummaging for a sweater. There was a chill in the house that the laboring furnace couldn't eliminate. The warm spell had ended, and now winter was trying to make up for its short vacation.

Marsha shoved a tangle of sweaters into the corner of her drawer. Her fingers touched a book at the bottom, and she pulled it out. She looked at the cover—padded, red plastic with the words My Diary inscribed in swirly, gold letters. It had been a present from Aunt Laura for her last birthday.

Marsha unhooked the clasp. She had never bothered to lock it, although she had spent some time deciding on the perfect hiding place for the tiny gold key. She'd finally selected the third bookshelf and had set the key on her worn copy of The Black Stallion.

Her plan had been to move the key to other books at least once a week—from its present hiding place to Tales of a Fourth Grade Nothing to Tuck Everlasting to Ramona and Her Father. But she had only made two dull entries in the diary, so there had never been any need to insure secrecy.

Aunt Laura had written a short message on the cover page. Her handwriting was bold and large and hard to read.

> To my darling, favorite, one and only niece on her
> eleventh birthday. Here's a place to keep all your
> lovely, exciting, and secret thoughts. I hope you have
> a wonderful year and life!! Your loving aunt— Laura

Marsha bit her lip thoughtfully. She suddenly slammed her drawer shut, forgetting a sweater, and grabbed a pen off her cluttered desk. She plopped down onto her bed and pulled the extra blanket over her knees. Flipping pages she found a blank one. Without even bothering to skim her first entries, she began to write.

January 8
Dear Diary,

Last summer I wrote about getting a sister. Then I thought it was sort of a neat idea. I'd be more like Rosie. She always has somebody to play with—even when she doesn't want to. Me—I've just got my parents and J.J. (Jumpin' Jehosephat), my cat.

A social worker—Mrs. Daniels— came to our place about six times to talk with us about adopting a little girl. I had to clean my room over and over even though she only peeked at it once!

It was kind of exciting though, thinking and dreaming about my new sister. For a while it seemed that was all we talked about at our house. Then, finally, the report on our family was done. It's called a home study. So now we've been waiting and waiting. A year! Maybe more. I was starting to think we'd never get a kid.

Anyhow, tonight when I came in from feeding Butterscotch, Kate had a cup of cocoa all ready for me—with marshmallows. We hardly ever have marshmallows.

It felt like we were some family on T.V.—all sitting around real cozy. I started thinking about Mike Adams. I liked him last year—maybe I still do. Anyhow, he calls me Marsha Marshmallow.

Then Kate ruined it. She started talking about the adoption and how it's taking longer than expected and how they want another kid so very much.

David said that lots of people adopt healthy, normal babies and young children. But some kids wait and wait for a home.

Guess what? My parents want to adopt a kid who's been waiting—a kid other families might not want. They told me they want a little girl with a handicap.

When they said that, I took a gulp of cocoa and burned my tongue. Finally, I asked, "What sort of handicap?"

Kate said, "Oh, deaf, blind, but probably developmentally delayed." She went on and talked about how she used to teach kids like that when she lived in Philadelphia. Now Mom's a reading specialist. She teaches kids who have trouble reading.

At first the words "developmentally delayed" threw me off, then it hit me. Retarded! That's what they meant! Like the kids in the special ed class at my school.

Then David asked me how I felt about having a sister like that, and I didn't know what to say. I sort of mumbled something like, "It'd be okay." I drank my cocoa and went to bed fast.

Now I don't know what to do. I don't understand why my parents want a retarded kid, or any other kid. Don't they think having me is good enough? I've never made any trouble for them. I think we have a happy family. We don't talk a lot about how we feel and stuff like that, but we get along *pretty well—a lot better than Rosie's family does.*

It's strange. I've known my parents all my life, but I don't know how to tell them how I really feel. I'm kind of afraid to admit that I don't <u>ever</u> want a retarded sister! If I tell them, they'll be upset. They'll think I'm being selfish.

But I don't care if some stupid little kid needs parents. Why does she need <u>my</u> parents?

I think I'll be writing lots more in this diary, and I'm going to start locking it. For sure!

Marsha sat back with a sigh. Her hand ached from holding her pen so tightly, but writing everything down had been even better than talking to a friend. Nibbling her thumbnail, she read the last few sentences she'd written in the diary and then added,

Sincerely,
Marsha O'Dell.

4

"Our new social worker is coming Friday afternoon," Kate announced at breakfast on Wednesday. "So, David, please be sure to be home on time. You don't have a yearbook meeting, do you?"

Marsha's father shook his head. "Not on Friday. I'll be here. Don't worry, Honey."

There was a tense expression on her mother's pale face that Marsha couldn't help noticing.

"I just have a gut feeling that this is it," Kate said. I think Ms. Kerp, that's her name, is going to have a little girl for us."

"You mean, have a kid with her?" Marsha asked hoarsely.

"No, no. Just that maybe she'll tell us about a child. One who's ready to be adopted."

"Oh," said Marsha, her voice dull and flat. Her parents didn't seem aware of her unenthusiastic reaction.

Friday afternoon arrived on schedule. The whole family

waited expectantly in the freshly cleaned living room for the new social worker to arrive.

Marsha gnawed her right thumbnail carefully. She didn't want to bite off too much. Her left thumbnail was already chewed down to the quick. For the past year she'd been trying to stop biting her nails, so she'd limited herself to just her thumbs, and it worked. If she remembered to hide her thumbs, the rest of her nails looked presentable.

Kate leaped up from the chair next to the fireplace and began to straighten the cushions on the couch.

"Relax, Honey," David said gently. "We've been through all this before with Mrs. Daniels."

"I know. But I hate meeting new people. It always makes me nervous. Just wish Mrs. Daniels hadn't retired and moved to Florida. She was such a nice, easygoing person."

Marsha watched her mother sit down and cross her legs. Usually, Kate gave the impression of being in control of situations. Her short-cropped, reddish-blond hair and slender, athletic body gave her a strong, confident air. Marsha was mildly surprised to hear Kate's confession of nervousness.

With her hands folded neatly in her lap and her thumbs hidden, Marsha tried to relax. She didn't want to meet a new social worker, either, and the longer she sat, the more anxious she felt.

A new worker and a new kid, too; that was the problem. While talking to Mrs. Daniels, Marsha had pictured a cute little girl who would be thrilled with a pony to ride. They would have ridden together, Marsha on her handsome new horse and her adorable new sister following on Butterscotch. But that image was gone now, replaced by a vague, troubling idea of a retarded kid.

Marsha thought, I wonder if it was this Ms. Kerp lady who convinced Mom and Dad to get a retarded kid. If she did, I hate her.

"Here she is! I'm just going to check the tea water," Kate said and then dashed off into the kitchen.

"Why does she have to do that now?" Marsha asked. Her father shrugged his shoulders and gave her a reassuring grin. Marsha sighed and thought, I suppose she'll be off fussing with tea bags while I'm left out here to meet Ms. Kerp—burp. Ms. Kerp burps.

Marsha glanced out the window at the attractive young woman coming up the front walk. Was she really burping? Could be.

The doorbell rang, but Marsha pretended to be engrossed in a magazine. David answered it.

"Hello!" Ms. Kerp said brightly. "You must be Mr. O'Dell. I'm so glad to meet you."

"David. Just call me David."

"Certainly, David it is. Feels like winter again out there."

"We were all spoiled by that warm spell," David said as he took her coat and offered her a chair. Marsha stood up uncertainly.

"And you're Martha, right?" Ms. Kerp smiled pleasantly.

"Glad to meet you," Marsha said and plopped back down, the magazine still clutched in her hand.

"You're almost right," her father told the social worker. "This is our daughter, Marsha."

Just remember marshmallows, Marsha thought, then you won't forget. And I'll keep burps in mind so I'll never forget your name.

She gave Ms. Kerp a relaxed smile.

"Marsha! That's it," said the social worker. "I'm sorry. I'm not very good with names."

"Kate! Ms. Kerp's here," David called.

J.J. sauntered into the room and stretched. He began to purr and twine himself around Ms. Kerp's legs.

"Nice kitty," she said, reaching down and shoving at him. Marsha felt a trace of amusement. This new social worker was showing signs of being a cat hater. With a gentle mew, J.J. leaped lightly into Ms. Kerp's lap.

"Oh!" she exclaimed with no brightness at all.

"Marsha, how about if you take J.J. upstairs and put him in your room?" David suggested in his firm schoolteacher tone.

Marsha rose slowly and replaced her magazine in the rack before rescuing Ms. Kerp. The cat was already kneading her lap contentedly and had left several of his white hairs on her dark skirt.

On her way to her room, Marsha took her time. She was in no hurry to return to the strained atmosphere in the living room. She dragged her feet in the hallway, hoping to make a squeak on the shiny wood floor.

Inside her room she shut the door and set J.J. on the top bunk. She glanced around. Everything looked clean and neat in honor of Ms. Kerp's visit—except maybe the model horses, which really needed dusting. Marsha blew on their plastic and ceramic backs, and a satisfyingly noticeable cloud rose above their manes and tails.

Marsha put her head closer and peered at the face of her Arabian stallion. She'd named him Ransome. Would her new horse look like him?

J.J. took a flying leap from the bed to the horse shelf, knocking over several colts.

"You goof!" Marsha scolded him. He purred and picked his way toward her, avoiding the mares and stallions. "Get off, Jumpin' Jehosephat." He bounded down with a flick of his tail.

The colts needed to be helped back onto their feet. Marsha began to make up a story as she rearranged the models. A white mountain lion had chased the youngest foal. Frantically, the foal leaped a gully, tumbled, and fell. The stallion heard his cry of distress and galloped to the rescue, mane and tail whipped by the mountain wind.

Just then, Kate called for Marsha to come down. With a sigh of regret, she left her room, shutting the mountain lion in with his prey.

When she reached the living room, she discovered her parents had both gone into the kitchen, shutting the door behind them.

"Marsha," Ms. Kerp said, "I need to ask you a few questions." Marsha perched uneasily on the edge of the couch. "How do you feel about getting a new sister?"

Marsha shrugged her shoulders. "Okay, I guess."

"Are you excited?" Ms. Kerp tilted her head slightly, and Marsha was tempted to imitate her.

"Yeah, sort of. I'd like a sister I can do stuff with." She

hesitated. "Mrs. Daniels asked me lots of questions last year."

The social worker smiled as she spoke, revealing perfect white teeth. "As a matter of fact, she did. And she reported that she felt you'd be very receptive to having a sibling join your family. I just want to go over some things. Now, I understand your parents have discussed with you their plans to adopt a handicapped child."

Marsha nodded, "We've talked about it a little bit. I . . . I just don't know what a kid like that would be like, I guess." Marsha shrugged.

"Developmentally delayed children are like all kids," said Ms. Kerp. "They're just behind. They act younger than they really are. And, Marsha, your parents are not asking for a severely delayed child."

Marsha nodded and managed to smile. She felt trapped and wanted to get this interview over as soon as possible. Finally, Ms. Kerp said pleasantly, "Well, let's call your parents back in, all right?"

Marsha sprang from her seat and went to the kitchen door. "She wants you back," Marsha told her parents. David gave her a quick smile and said to the social worker as he returned to his chair in the living room, "I think we're all unsure of what it'll be like sharing our lives with a little stranger."

"I can certainly understand that," said Ms. Kerp. "Having another child in your home is going to mean a lot of changes in your family. There'll be ongoing adjustments for each of you. And there is no certain way to predict how things will work out. But it's best for everyone to have a positive attitude and to assume that the placement is permanent, even though it'll be six months before the adoption can be made official in court."

Six months, thought Marsha. Those six months will be a trial period, and then the kid can go back to wherever she came from.

"Now, could we go into the dining room?" Ms. Kerp asked as she stood up.

"Oh, yes. Please do. I have tea and cookies all ready," Kate said quickly.

"I just need a flat surface to put some papers on, and I did bring a picture to show you."

"A picture of a child? Wonderful!" Kate's voice was high with excitement.

Marsha chomped her thumbnail as she followed her parents into the dining room.

The picture Ms. Kerp placed on the table looked like a school portrait. A smiling face gazed up at Marsha—a little girl with white-blond hair and dark brown eyes. Marsha frowned. This child didn't look at all like a retarded kid to Marsha.

"Her name is Wendy," said Ms. Kerp.

"Wendy," Kate whispered. "She's just beautiful."

"Yes, she's a real little pixie." Ms. Kerp smiled. "I've known Wendy for years but haven't seen her for the past eight or nine months. I worked with her shortly after she first came into foster care."

"You mean she's been adopted before?" asked Marsha.

Ms. Kerp shook her head. "No. Foster homes are seldom permanent. A child in foster care doesn't legally belong to the foster family. Often kids are moved around quite a bit. However, agencies are trying to prevent that from happening because all children need stability."

"What else do you know about Wendy?" asked David.

"Well, she was about three when I met her. She's had a difficult life. Her birthmother was very young and unmarried when Wendy was born. She tried her best to parent Wendy but couldn't manage. I don't think she was mature enough to deal with any child, let alone one with special needs. Wendy has been in various foster homes ever since she was about one and a half years old. During those years her mother made some attempt at maintaining contact. Then, about two years ago, her birthmother married, and her husband totally refused to take Wendy into their home and life. Six months ago, when she gave birth to a son, her birthmother agreed to an adoption plan for Wendy. Now Wendy is free to be adopted."

"Does she remember her mother?" asked Kate.

"I honestly don't know. Wendy's eight years old now. In the past her contact with her birthmother has been very brief and sporadic. Wendy's lived in six different foster homes. Just last month she had to be uprooted again because her foster family moved out of state. Her present social worker would like to get her placed in an adoptive home as soon as possible. I think the foster mother is having some health problems. She has five foster children and can't keep any of them much longer."

Ms. Kerp began to collect her papers. "I'll leave the picture with you. Give me a call if you decide you'd like to meet Wendy and later go over her file in detail. If you do decide to parent her, you'll want to know about her life history."

"What do you think, David?" Kate asked.

"It's fine with me if we just set up the meeting time right now," he answered.

Marsha stared at her father. She felt a strange hollow sensation somewhere inside. How could this be happening so fast? I am not ready for this, she thought. No way!

"Now, one more word of caution," said Ms. Kerp. "Just remember that Wendy acts quite a bit younger than her age. In many ways she's more like a four-year-old and in some ways a two-year-old."

"We understand," Kate said, nodding.

"I just have a feeling you will be the right family for Wendy. I'm sure Mrs. Daniels would agree with me." Ms. Kerp was all smiles.

Well, thought Marsha as she took another nibble of her nail, goody-goody for Mrs. Daniels. She's off enjoying the warm Florida sunshine while I'm here getting ready to meet some little brat. Wendy . . . I wonder what she'll be like?

5

This is unreal, Marsha thought. She couldn't quite believe they were driving off to meet the kid in the picture that was hanging on the bulletin board in the kitchen. Marsha had studied the small portrait for a week, yet the child still seemed as distant as a character in a book. Actually, Marsha felt she'd have been much more excited and pleased about meeting Beverly Cleary's Ramona, or Ken from *My Friend Flicka,* or even the Wendy from *Peter Pan.* Meeting them would not have been any more weird than this trip to see a real live retarded kid that might become her sister.

The drive took them through farmland and towns and eventually into the city. Marsha gazed out the window at the pollution-grayed buildings and trash-trimmed gutters. There were no people on the windy corners. Only the dancing litter indicated that humans were responsible for the landscape.

Marsha was relieved when they drove on and came to a

pleasant area with trees growing along the sidewalks, their trunks protected by cylindrical wrought iron guards.

"We're almost there," her father said as he glanced at the map sent to them by Wendy's foster mother.

Marsha swallowed and wished she'd eaten more than half an apple for breakfast. Her stomach was empty to the point of aching.

"Nervous, Honey?" Her mother looked back at Marsha.

"I guess so. Maybe I'm just hungry."

David chuckled. "Me, too. We'll go out to eat with Wendy. Ah . . . here we are. There's Ms. Kerp's car."

"What's she doing here?" Marsha asked abruptly.

Kate answered, "Wendy's social worker is out of town. She asked Ms. Kerp to be at this first meeting since she knows Wendy."

The house was a brick duplex. As Marsha followed her parents up the steps, she noticed that the small front yard was a mass of tangled vines. Several toys—a green water pistol, a brownish ball, three or four Lego blocks—were trapped beneath the dead-looking, intertwined stems.

The front porch was enclosed, but even before the door was opened, Marsha could see that it was used for storage. Cardboard boxes were piled against the smudged windows.

Ms. Kerp answered David's knock, wearing her customary, bright smile. "Welcome! Come in and meet Mrs. Johnson."

As she walked through the porch, Marsha stepped carefully to avoid tripping over a capsized tricycle. This house reminded her of Rosie's.

A strong odor of cooking food permeated the air, and Marsha's stomach began to growl. She folded her arms across her waist and pressed hard, trying to quiet her insides. From across the living room, four small children regarded her. They were sitting on a worn couch, their feet sticking out awkwardly. Each of them had short-cropped dark hair and wore jeans and brightly printed T-shirts. They squirmed and giggled, but didn't say a word. A large color television mumbled from its prominent place against one wall. Next to it stood a bird cage. Marsha couldn't see a bird.

Mrs. Johnson, their foster mother, was a tall, heavyset woman with wispy grey hair. She extended a large hand and greeted Marsha's parents.

"I'm so glad to meet you, Mr. and Mrs. O'Dell. And you must be Wendy's new sister. Wendy's real excited. I've tried my best to explain things to her, but I'm not sure I've got through to her."

"Wendy has only been here a few weeks," Ms. Kerp explained. "So she's not completely settled in, nor has Mrs. Johnson had much chance to get to know her."

"Oh, we know her well enough!" Mrs. Johnson gave a deep-throated laugh. "Right, kids?" She nodded at the four children who grinned and poked at each other. "Tanya, would you go up and get Wendy?"

Mrs. Johnson turned to Ms. Kerp and added, "She's been hiding in a closet most of the morning. At least I managed to get her dressed."

"Wendy has had a lot of changes in her life," Ms. Kerp said. "So we have to expect her to react in some way."

"Oh, she reacts, all right!" said Mrs. Johnson.

"She like to scream," one of the children offered.

"Yeah. She's loud!" another added.

Marsha felt as if the room were becoming smaller and more crowded. She reached out and grabbed her father's hand. He gave it a reassuring squeeze.

"Ah, here's the little princess. Cute as a button. It was Tanya there who helped me pick out those clothes," said Mrs. Johnson. Her booming voice seemed to fill the room.

Tanya hung onto Wendy's hand and dragged her halfway across the floor. Then she returned to her spot on the couch, leaving Wendy alone in the middle of the room with her head down.

Marsha stared at the little girl. She was dressed in a bright pink shirt, stiff new jeans, and white sneakers that had pink laces.

"Hi, Wendy," Marsha's mother said carefully as she stepped over to her and knelt down. Wendy turned her head to one side, avoiding eye contact.

"We're going to take you out to eat," Kate continued in the same soft tone of voice as she gently parted Wendy's long bangs to reveal dark eyes.

"Out?" Wendy whispered. "Eat?"

"That's how I got her to come down," Tanya said. "I just told her some real nice people is here to take her out to eat. She just loves to eat."

Mrs. Johnson chuckled. "Yes, she sure does. I must say, though, she can be mighty fussy sometimes. She sure knows what she likes and is stuck on those foods."

Okay, okay, let's get out of here, Marsha thought.

"Well, I think we're all set," David said briskly in his teacher's voice.

Waving and saying good-bye, they made their way to the car. Marsha noticed the expressions of longing on the other foster kids' faces. She wondered why they had to live in a foster home.

Marsha sat next to Wendy in the back seat. She was relieved that Wendy could talk and looked normal, just sitting and staring out the car window. Marsha glanced at the little girl and decided she was even prettier than her picture. Golden hair that reached almost to her waist hung loosely down her back. Not a ribbon nor a barrette held it in check. Her brown eyes were huge in her pale face. Her hands were clasped in her lap, and Marsha noticed that her arms looked wiry but strong.

No marshmallow here, Marsha thought.

She smiled tentatively at Wendy, who was now staring at her. "Hi, I'm Marsha. Where would you like to go out to eat?"

"Mar-da?" Wendy said slowly.

For a second Marsha didn't know what she meant.

"Oh," she said. "You mean my name? It's Mar-sha. Can you say it like that?"

Wendy shook her head quickly and turned away.

"I saw some fast food places not far from here," David said. "I'll just drive along, and if you girls see a place that strikes your fancy, give me a holler."

Marsha was glad it only took a few minutes to find a restaurant. She didn't have any idea what to say to Wendy.

"I hope it's not too crowded," Kate said, peering out the window while running a comb through her hair. She turned to the girls and commented, "Well, you two certainly look nice. Almost like sisters already."

Ah, come off it, Mom, Marsha thought. Let's face it, she's prettier than I am—even if she is retarded.

Inside the restaurant they chose a booth in the corner. Wendy slid behind the table and immediately grabbed the ketchup bottle.

Kate's voice was pleasant but firm as she said, "No, not yet Wendy. See? Daddy's going to get us some food. Then you can have some ketchup."

"Here," Marsha said, grasping the bottle at its base. "I'll put it right in the middle so we can all reach it." She pulled it gently away, but Wendy jerked hard on the bottle. As she yanked it toward herself, Wendy's hands slipped upward, lifting off the bottle cap. The ketchup sloshed out onto her clean shirt, between her fingers, and down onto her jeans.

"I'm sorry," Marsha said quickly. She tried to wipe the ketchup off with a napkin, but the little girl giggled and twisted away.

"I'll take her to the rest room," her mother said. "Come on, Wendy. Let's see what the bathroom looks like."

Wendy frowned and touched her T-shirt with one finger, then she licked off a dab of ketchup. She didn't seem the slightest bit interested in going with Kate.

Hope she doesn't start screaming, Marsha thought.

Kate held out her hand. Marsha felt the tension ease when Wendy grabbed it and went off quietly.

Marsha pushed the ketchup bottle back to the center of the table and leaned against the slightly sticky orange seat.

"Where is everybody?" David asked as he arrived carrying a tray heaped with food in paper bags and drinks in paper cups.

"Wendy got ketchup on herself, so Mom's cleaning her up."

"Oh, well, those things happen. I got you a super-duper burger. You like those, right?"

"Yeah. All except the tomato."

"I'll eat it for you," her father offered.

Marsha took a huge bite of her hamburger. She watched the door to the rest room anxiously. Finally, after what seemed like half an hour, her mother and Wendy emerged. Kate's face was flushed, yet her expression was satisfied. She held Wendy's hand, but with a sharp yank Wendy was free to hop back to her seat. She looked huge, leaping up and down next to the table when she saw all the food.

Marsha stuffed the rest of her burger into her mouth and took a gulp of cold soda. The food was settling to the bottom of her stomach where it felt like one solid lump.

"Are you hungry, Wendy?" David asked.

Why ask? Marsha wondered. Wendy was already rummaging through the packages of food and shoving French fries into her mouth faster than she could chew them. When she located a hamburger, she picked it up, pulled the bun apart, and sniffed the pickle.

"Wendy, just eat your food," said Kate.

"Watch out for the ketchup," Marsha said as Wendy grabbed the bottle again. David offered to help her, but she frowned and shook her head so vigorously that her hair stood almost straight out from her head.

"Okay, be careful," said David.

Just as Wendy poured half a cup of ketchup on her hamburger, a young couple with their small son and baby came and sat down across the aisle. The boy looked about five years old. He glanced at Wendy and grinned broadly when he saw her put the bun back on her burger. The ketchup squished out, leaving a red ring on the paper wrapping.

"There goes the shirt again," Kate muttered while dabbing with a napkin at the oozing bun.

"Mmmmm," Wendy said with a satisfied smile, her mouth stuffed.

Marsha slid farther and farther down in her seat, wishing she could keep on going all the way onto the floor and then melt away.

"She's messy," the little boy whispered loudly to his mother.

The baby in his high chair began to bang the metal tray with his fist. Wendy stopped slurping her drink and stared at him, then she grinned and started to bang the table. The baby giggled, and Wendy laughed loudly.

"She's silly!" announced the boy.

Wendy tossed her head, sending her hair flopping and flying through the air. Suddenly she ducked under the table, stuck her head out, and yelled, "Boo!"

The baby clapped his chubby hands and laughed.

"That's enough, Wendy," said Kate. "Have you finished all your food?" Kate checked through the mess on the table. She uncovered several French fries which Wendy snatched and jammed into her mouth while she scrambled back into her seat.

"Time to go," David said firmly.

Marsha got up thankfully and struggled into her coat. She felt unbearably warm already but was so embarrassed that she wanted to hide inside something.

"No!" Wendy's voice carried all over the restaurant. She gripped the edge of the table with both hands. "Me stay!"

"Oh, boy," Kate whispered.

The family across the aisle got up and moved to another table.

David reached for Wendy's arm, but as soon as he touched her, she shook her head frantically.

Then it began—the screaming. Marsha stood uncertainly for a few moments feeling pinned, held motionless by the stares of the other people who had stopped eating to watch the blond child act like a spoiled toddler.

I'm not her sister! Marsha wanted to yell. She doesn't belong with us!

Marsha waited another second while she tried not to look at Wendy's tear-streaked face and screaming, distorted mouth. Then Marsha fled to the car, not caring that she was deserting her parents.

She sat rigidly in the seat, trying not to think or feel anything. She stared at the chrome door handle, willing herself to be like the inanimate object—still, numb, and cold. Wendy's screams soon announced her arrival. David opened the door, plopped her down, and buckled her seat belt. Marsha scooted as far away from the thrashing, screaming child as she could.

"We've got to fasten her seat belt," Kate said above the shrieks.

"I already did," said David as he climbed into the driver's seat.

"Good!" said Kate. "She has to know that we have rules right from the beginning." Kate's mouth was set in a determined line.

Wendy continued to jab her toes against the front seat while slamming her head against the back of her own seat. Her screams and tears diminished. By the time they reached the foster home, she had quit crying. She gazed out the window, her eyes red and her lashes fringed with tears.

"You're home," Kate said gently.

"No." Wendy's voice was soft and hoarse. "No home."

Reluctantly, she got out of the car and walked slowly up the steps holding Kate's hand.

"Some kid," David said as though talking to himself. "She's got lots of spunk."

Marsha glared down at her tightly clenched hands. Her knuckles were white, and she felt like chewing her nails—all of them.

Spunk? That's one way to put it, she thought.

"Well, what do you think?" Kate asked when she returned to the car.

"She's a cute little girl," David said. "How do you feel?"

Marsha sat silently, listening to her parents talk as if they'd forgotten she was there.

"I think Wendy has lots of potential. We must remember that she's had a really tough time. Maybe we can help her."

Who can help her? Marsha thought angrily. Not me, I don't even want her.

David said, "Wendy would be a lot of fun and a real challenge. By the way, that little lunch brought back memories. Remember the time we took Marsha out to eat and she stood up on her seat?"

Kate laughed. "And she spilled soda all over the man in the booth behind us!"

"But how old was I? I don't even remember," Marsha blurted.

"You must have been about three," her father said.

Kate turned and looked at Marsha with a direct and loving expression which held her daughter still.

"You have to understand, Honey. Wendy is developmentally delayed. She's going to act younger than she is. She'll never really grow up, at least not like you will. Yet, with extra help, she can learn a lot. We could help her and so could you."

Marsha gave a quick nod and turned her head toward the window so that her mother would not see the look of dismay on her face.

6

January 23
Dear Diary,
We met Wendy last weekend. It was awful. She's like
a giant baby. But that doesn't really describe her.
Funny thing is, she's really pretty and doesn't look
retarded, but she sure acts like she is.

I thought maybe Kate and David would say
forget it. But no. They seem like they really want her.
What are they trying to prove? I don't understand
them at all!

Dad's sister, my Aunt Laura, is mad. She
called the day after we met Wendy. She lives in New
York City in this fantastic apartment with plants all

over and modern paintings practically covering the walls and rugs so thick you feel like you're walking on fuzzy sponge rubber. She's co-owner of a shop that sells antiques and paintings.

Anyhow—I picked up the phone upstairs, just as Mom answered it in the kitchen. I couldn't resist listening! It was sort of like a play—only they didn't know about the audience—me! The conversation went something like this:

Aunt Laura: Hello, Kate, dear. I just had to call. I hope you and David aren't going to go ahead with that foolish plan of yours.
Kate: What plan?
Aunt Laura: The one you wrote to me about— adopting a retarded child. (She says "retarded" the same way she says "fat"—like it's some deadly disease!)
Kate: As a matter of fact, we are planning to adopt her. We've met Wendy, and will be bringing her home soon.
Aunt Laura: I certainly hope you haven't made any unrealistic promises to some do-gooder social worker. I just think you and David are too idealistic. You don't know what you're getting yourselves into!
Kate: You seem to have forgotten that I taught developmentally delayed children like Wendy for several years. I know, Laura, that you can't understand us, but it's what we both want to do.

Well, Aunt Laura went on and on about how this adoption would ruin our lives. She sure was convincing! She even said that adopting Wendy would be bad for me. She said I was smart and attractive (even she's too honest to call me pretty) and that Wendy would take up so much of my parents' time they wouldn't have any left for me.

I don't remember what Mom answered to that. Something about how having a sister like Wendy would help me grow up to be a better person. I don't know—maybe I should run away to New York and live with Aunt Laura. She might let me bring J.J. along, but I'd miss Mom and Dad, I think. And I know I'd miss Rosie and Butterscotch.

It's getting late, and I have school tomorrow.

Your friend,
Marsha

P.S. I told Rosie that I'm writing in my diary, and she wants to see it. But I'm never going to let her or anybody else read it. It's just for me. I have to decide which book to put the key on tonight.

P.P.S. I told Rosie about Wendy, too. At first she said I should make a big scene and convince my parents that getting Wendy was a terrible idea. But then, when I showed her Wendy's picture, she said, "Gee, she's really cute. Maybe she won't be so bad." And then when I told her all about our lunch with Wendy, she just said, "Sounds like my little sisters. You've been spoiled, Marsha, never having to put up with kids younger than you!"

With friends like that who needs enemies?

January 27
Dear Diary,
I can't believe it. Wendy's here! She's asleep—
finally—on my bottom bunk. Guess who had to move
up on top! J.J. is curled up almost on Wendy's face.
Maybe he'll smother her.

We went to get her today. Mrs. Johnson,
Wendy's foster mother, has to go in the hospital for
some big operation. So it all happened fast. Too fast!

The drive there took forever, and by the time we
got to the foster home, I really had to go to the
bathroom—bad. I felt sort of stupid asking to use
theirs. So I waited until we were on the way home
and told Dad. He was not very happy, but we
stopped at a gas station. Wendy was sitting real
still. She was hanging onto her little suitcase like it
was the only thing she had in the world. Which, I
guess, is true. Anyhow, Mom (Kate) asked her if
she had to go to the potty. She just shook her head no
the way she does with her hair flying out.

After we got going again and were out on the
highway, Wendy started crying, and I smelled
something. Sure enough, she had pooped in her pants!

Kate was afraid Wendy'd have one of her
screaming fits if we stopped and tried to clean her
up. So we drove all the way home with this awful
smell in the car. We rolled the windows down
partway, and Dad turned the heater way up. But I
could still smell it.

When we got home Mom gave Wendy a bath
and put clean clothes on her. She found one of my old
snowsuits and helped Wendy put it on. Then I took

her out to the pasture to meet Butterscotch. I asked her if she liked ponies, and she nodded.

But maybe she thought I said puppies because as soon as she saw Butterscotch her eyes got real big, and her face got even whiter than usual. I helped her climb up onto the top rail of the fence, and then I led Butterscotch over to her. Wendy sat there like she was frozen solid with fear. He put his nose out and pushed her a little, just a nudge, the way he does to me when he wants a treat.

That stupid kid fell right off the fence! She went over backwards. Good thing she had that fat suit on with the hood up. Of course, she acted like I'd tried to kill her. She screamed and ran all the way back to the house.

I tried to tell Kate what had happened, but she just looked annoyed and kept fussing over Wendy. She even held her in the rocking chair and sang her some songs. Wendy looked so silly with her legs hanging way down almost to the floor.

I don't know how I'll teach Wendy to ride if she's afraid of Butterscotch. I can't believe she's eight years old. She doesn't talk very well. Some words, like my name, she really messes up. She calls me Mar-da.

I am very tired. This has been the longest, worst day of my life. The day we met Wendy was almost as bad. If it keeps up like this, I'll feel like I'm ninety by the time I'm twelve. My birthday is in June after school lets out.

I'd better quit writing. Tomorrow's Sunday, and then the next day Wendy starts school. I can hardly wait. Hah!!

Your friend,
Marsha— not Marda!

7

Marsha woke with a vague sense of uneasiness as though she'd had a bad dream but couldn't quite remember it. Then her eyes popped open, and she sat up.

Oh, no. Wendy!

She leaned over and peered down into the bottom bunk. It was empty, except for a mass of tangled blankets. The pillow was on the floor. There was no sign of J.J. Marsha glanced at her clock. Seven o'clock!

It's late, she thought in a moment of panic. Then she remembered that her father had promised to drive her and Wendy to school because it was Wendy's first day.

The night before, Marsha had argued that it would be much better for Wendy if she stayed home a few days.

"She's not really used to us yet, Mom. Starting school is going to be really tough for her."

"We've discussed this with Ms. Kerp," Kate told her. "She feels it's best for Wendy to get right into a regular routine. And I've talked to Mrs. Fisher. She'll be Wendy's teacher, except for when Wendy is mainstreamed into the regular classes. I was impressed with Mrs. Fisher, and she's looking forward to meeting and working with Wendy."

Boy, is she in for a surprise, Marsha thought.

Marsha climbed down off her bunk. She put on the first clothes she pulled out of her drawer, ran a brush through her hair, and glared in the mirror. Then she stuck out her tongue at herself and ran downstairs.

Breakfast was a delicious spread of pancakes, sausage, orange juice, and mixed fruit. Marsha noticed that meals had shown a definite improvement since Wendy's arrival.

Wonder how long Mom can keep this up, Marsha thought as she looked at all the food. Last night we had yummy roast chicken and all the trimmings. Who cares that Wendy only ate the stuffing?

Everyone else was already in the kitchen. Wendy looked perky and precious. She was dressed in a pair of bib overalls and a long-sleeved shirt with tiny red hearts all over it.

"Where'd she get that outfit?" Marsha asked.

"I bought it last week," Kate said while she forked pancakes onto Wendy's plate. "I didn't know whether she'd have any good school clothes, so I got her several new things. I needed an excuse to check out that new discount store on the edge of Richville."

"I need new sneakers." Marsha looked at her father as she said this. He often took her shopping after school.

"Okay," he said with his mouth full. He chewed a moment and swallowed. "But didn't I just buy you a pair?"

"Those are for gym, Daddy. I have to leave them at school. I need some to wear every day."

"What about boots? It's cold out. Too cold for sneakers," Kate said.

"Nobody wears boots, Mom, not unless there's a huge snow-storm. Can't I just have a new pair of sneakers without a fuss?" Marsha frowned. If she hadn't felt a twinge of jealousy, she probably wouldn't have mentioned the sneakers. How could she be jealous of Wendy? It didn't make a whole lot of sense.

"I'll get you some sneakers next weekend," David said.

Wendy continued to shovel pancakes into her mouth.

"Careful. You'll choke," Kate cautioned her.

Marsha poured a huge helping of syrup on her pancakes. The sausage tasted even more delicious when she used it to mop up the excess syrup.

If I keep eating like this, she thought, Mike'll have a good reason to call me Marshmallow.

Marsha glanced at Wendy who was eating with incredible concentration. Her whole body was hunched over her plate and its contents.

"It's almost time to go," David said. "I want to have a few minutes to get Wendy to her classroom. Girls, you had better get your breakfasts finished."

"More!" Wendy demanded, holding her plate aloft.

"Sorry, all gone, Honey. You had plenty. Six, wasn't it?" Kate said.

Wendy held both hands above her head, fingers spread, and shouted, "Ten!"

"Well, maybe," Kate said, looking doubtful. "But I hope not. You'll be sick at school with that much in your tummy."

Wendy grinned and patted her stomach.

"Better go wash your hands, Wendy. And don't forget to brush your teeth, too."

"She eats the toothpaste, Mom. I've seen her. You'd better go and supervise!"

"Oh, Marsha, could you help her, please? I'm just about to eat my own breakfast."

"Sure," Marsha felt a wave of resentment, but she got up and took Wendy by the hand. "Yuk. Wendy, your hands feel like they've been dipped in glue."

The handwashing, teeth brushing, and ride to school went well, despite Marsha's misgivings. She had been afraid that Wendy would wet her pants, or worse. She was also concerned about Wendy throwing a tantrum on the way into the school building.

Instead, Wendy took David's hand and walked quietly along

with him. She even waved to Marsha as she entered her own classroom.

The day went slowly for Marsha. In the excitement of Wendy's arrival, she'd forgotten all about a science report that was due that day. Usually Mrs. Swanson did not assign homework over the weekend, but this had been a big project involving research. The class had been given two weeks to complete the work. Not having that report ruined Marsha's entire day.

At lunchtime Marsha was glad to escape the classroom. She and Rosie sat with several other girls at one of the fold-down tables in the gym. When Marsha saw Mike sauntering over, she concentrated on her food, hoping to avoid his teasing.

"What's the matter, Marshmallow," Mike demanded. "Miss Perfect didn't do her homework, I hear. I didn't know retardation was contagious." He shoved his friend Rick, who was in Marsha's class, on the arm. Rick laughed right on cue.

Marsha stared at her tray of food. Rick must have told Mike about the science paper, but who had told him about Wendy? Her hot meal suddenly didn't look very appetizing.

"Bug off, Bird Brain," Rosie told him.

"Uh, oh! The bowwow is starting to bark. Is her bark worse than her bite?" Mike pretended to hide behind Rick for protection.

Rosie's tone was bantering when she said, "Wouldn't you like to know?" Some of the other girls began to giggle. Rick jumped behind Mike, grabbed his arm, and propelled him toward the exit.

As soon as the boys were out of earshot, Rosie turned to Marsha and whispered urgently, "Aren't you ever going to stand up to anybody? You know, Mike would be a good kid to practice on. Besides, he likes you, so you could be real mean to him and he wouldn't get mad."

"Oh, sure! He likes me. That's why he's so sweet to me," Marsha said sarcastically.

"I bet he does," one of the girls said. "Why else would he always be teasing you?"

"He is kind of cute, for a creep," added Allison, another sixth grader. "Isn't his mother Mexican or something? Gives him that tall, dark, and handsome look."

"Skip the tall part." Rosie giggled.

Marsha took a forkful of her mashed potatoes which tasted like the package they'd come in. She only half listened to the conversation around her. In the back of her mind she kept thinking one word over and over like some kind of chant. Wendy . . . Wendy . . .

Kate had arranged to leave work early so she could pick up the girls after school. "I think the bus ride would be too confusing for Wendy this first day," she'd told Marsha.

Although she had her own interests at heart, Marsha agreed with her mother. She was sure that by the end of the day, Mike would have a whole collection of obnoxious comments about Marsha and her retarded sister.

When the last bell finally rang, Marsha began to pack up her books carefully. Rosie rushed out of the classroom to the bus. Ol' Cranstram didn't like to wait for any latecomers.

"Marsha?" Her teacher's voice was stern. "What happened to your science report?"

Marsha looked up anxiously, "I . . . I forgot, Mrs. Swanson," she stammered. She felt her eyes beginning to smart and her face flush.

"You left it at home? Or you forgot to do it?" Mrs.Swanson persisted.

Marsha swallowed. "Sort of. I mean both. I had it almost finished last week. But I forgot about it over the weekend, and I didn't get it done." She had no intention of telling her teacher about Wendy. Mrs. Fisher had probably already filled her in anyway.

"You realize I'll have to mark your report down a grade for each day it's late." Although the teacher hadn't moved from behind her desk, Marsha had the feeling that she was bearing down on her. No wonder Mrs. Swanson had the reputation for being the toughest teacher in the school. "Just be certain to finish it tonight. I've been impressed with your ability, and I dislike having a talented student do poorly because of carelessness."

Marsha nodded, mumbled, "Bye," and hurried from the room.

Outside, the afternoon air felt refreshingly cold. Marsha took a deep breath, glad to be free of the overheated school building. She found Wendy on the sidewalk, hopping on one foot, then the other. Her teacher was with her, bundled in a down coat, holding Wendy's mittened hand.

"Hi, Mrs. Fisher," Marsha said.

"Hello. You must be Marsha. Wendy has been telling me what a nice new foster sister she has."

Marsha forced a smile. She wondered if Wendy had used the word foster or if her teacher just assumed that was the correct term.

"Hi! Hi, Mar-da!" Wendy said loudly as she tugged on Marsha's coat sleeve.

"Girls, I'd love to stand here and chat, but I have a heap of work to finish in my classroom. Bye, Wendy. Be sure to tell your mother what a nice day we had."

Wendy grinned and nodded vigorously. She clung to Marsha's sleeve.

Where's Mom? Marsha wondered uneasily as she peered up the street.

Then, turning to Wendy, she asked, "How was school? Was it as great as your teacher said?"

"Fun," Wendy responded quickly. She fumbled in her coat pocket and produced a rumpled piece of paper. "See? Me do name—Wendy."

Marsha stared at the wrinkled, smudged paper with its wobbly printing.

She's old enough for third grade and is just learning to write her name, Marsha thought with a sigh.

She squinted at an approaching green car. No, wrong driver.

"Hi, Marsha," a tall mature-looking girl with fluffy blond hair greeted Marsha.

"Oh, hi, Sharon." Marsha cringed inwardly. Sharon was in the other sixth grade class. Although they'd been together in fourth and fifth grades, they had never been friends.

"Did you miss your bus?" Sharon asked. She lived within walking distance of the school and often stayed late to help the teachers straighten desks and carry books to their cars.

"No. My mother's picking me up. She's a little late."

"She teaches in Richville, doesn't she? That's only about five miles from here," Sharon said.

"Yeah," said Marsha, wishing she could think of some clever way to get rid of the other girl.

"Hi!" Wendy exclaimed. Marsha wondered what had happened in school to turn up her volume.

Sharon glanced at Wendy but continued to address Marsha. "Your dad's a teacher over at the high school, isn't he? How come he can't pick you up?"

Marsha could just imagine how Rosie would have replied to such nosey questioning. She'd have said, "What's it to you?" But Marsha shrugged and replied, "They get out later. He has things going on after school, too. Plays, stuff like that. This year he's yearbook advisor."

"Oh, yeah? He teaches English, right?" Without waiting for a response, Sharon changed the subject. "Do you still have your little old pony? The one you used to talk about all the time."

"Yeah. But he's not old—only ten."

"Ten!" Wendy yelled and began counting on her fingers, yanking each finger up, one by one.

Marsha felt trapped. If only she'd used a Rosie put-down, maybe Sharon would be on her way home right now.

"Do you like Mr. James for a teacher?" Marsha asked quickly, hoping to distract Sharon from Wendy's display.

"Sure! He's neat. He tells lots of great stories. And he even laughs at Mike Adams sometimes. Remember how Mike used to act last year? Mrs. Wolf didn't think he was funny. Do you still like Mike?"

"My teacher Miss Fider," Wendy interrupted.

"What?" Sharon stared at Wendy.

"Mrs. Fisher," Marsha translated automatically.

"Oh." Sharon's eyes traveled over Wendy critically, as if she had just noticed her. "You're in *that* class."

Wendy grabbed Marsha's hand. "This new sissie," she said, her voice dropping to a whisper.

"Oh, sure, I bet!" Sharon laughed sarcastically. "They sure can act weird, can't they?"

Marsha's heart began to pound. A part of her wanted to pry Wendy's fingers loose and run away, but she stood still and gave Wendy's hand a slight squeeze.

"Who?" Marsha asked.

"Who what? Oh, you mean who's weird? You know! Those retards in Mrs. Fisher's room."

Marsha knew she should tell Sharon to shut up, but no words came. Her throat felt dry and tight, and her heart wouldn't calm down. She almost didn't notice her mother's car pulling up to the curb.

"We have to go now, bye." Marsha headed for the car, dragging Wendy. She was afraid to see Sharon's expression, so she didn't glance back.

8

"Please, Honey, sit in back with Wendy," Kate instructed as Marsha started to open the car's front door. With a sigh, Marsha plopped down next to Wendy in the back seat.

"How was your day, kids?"

"Miss Fider nice," Wendy announced. "But Ichie and Jadon mean!"

"The kids in your class sure have weird names," remarked Marsha.

Wendy's open, happy look changed immediately. She frowned fiercely, and her lower lip stuck out. "Weird! Retard! Not nice. Mean!" She was almost screaming.

Marsha was startled. She hadn't realized that Wendy had noticed or understood Sharon's remarks. "Sorry!" she said quickly. "I didn't mean that the kids are weird, Wendy. I guess maybe you just don't know their names too well. Let me guess. Is one named Richie and one Jason?"

Wendy's eyes narrowed in a guarded expression as she looked at Marsha, but she nodded slightly. Then, suddenly, she began to squirm and poke at her coat pocket.

"Me made Wendy," she said loudly. "Can't find!" Her voice rose higher while she searched frantically for her school paper.

"Here it is. You showed it to me, and I still have it." Marsha thrust the paper over the back of the seat to her mother.

"No! No!" Wendy shrieked. "Mine!"

"Geeze, okay," Marsha said. "I thought you wanted Mom to see it." She returned the school work to Wendy who grabbed it and scowled.

"May I see it, Wendy?" Kate asked quietly. Her tone of voice indicated that she thought there was no real problem in the back seat.

Wendy didn't answer. Her lower lip was beginning to tremble. Wisely, Kate changed the subject.

"What would you girls like for supper?"

"Hot dog!" yelled Wendy.

"Fried chicken," Marsha mumbled.

Kate said, "We've had hot dogs for lunch two days in a row—Saturday and Sunday. Isn't there something else you'd like tonight?"

"No! No! No!" Wendy chanted, punctuating each negative with a clunk of her heels. Marsha could feel the thuds on her side of the car's seat.

"Well, I suppose, if we have a big salad and some vegetables, hot dogs won't be too bad for us."

"You're starting to sound like Aunt Laura," Marsha remarked.

"There's nothing wrong with her advice on good nutrition," Kate said. "But some of her helpful hints I could do without."

She swung the car into the supermarket parking lot and began searching for a space.

Marsha wondered whether Aunt Laura had called again, but decided not to ask. "We can wait in the car," she suggested.

"Me wan' in! In! In!" Wendy shouted.

"You can both come inside," Kate said cheerfully as she

pulled into a parking space near the front entrance of the store.

"But, Mom . . ." Marsha muttered.

Wendy was already scrambling out of the car.

When they got into the store, Marsha regretted that she had not insisted on waiting in the car. Wendy ran off down the produce aisle. Within a few seconds she grabbed a peach and pressed it against her nose, inhaling deeply and loudly.

" 'Mell good!" she exclaimed when Marsha caught up with her.

"Put it back," Marsha ordered, grabbing for Wendy's free hand. "Just look. Don't touch," she whispered loudly.

"Mmmmm . . ." Wendy took another deep whiff of the peach. "Good! Wan' bite, Marda?"

"No!" Marsha's voice was now as loud as Wendy's. "No bites," she continued, trying to sound calm and firm. "Let's go get some more peaches in one of these plastic bags. We'll put them in the shopping cart."

At the word *cart*, Wendy tossed the peach back on the pile and raced up the aisle. She grabbed Kate's cart with one hand and pointed to the toddler's seat with the other.

"Wendy," Kate said patiently. "I think you're too big. That's for itty-bitty kids."

Marsha finished shoving the bruised peach under the healthy ones and turned to watch her mother and Wendy. They looked like any other mother and daughter with their similar coloring and slender builds.

"Mommy! Put me in!" The little girl's demanding words carried well in the large space of the market.

Uh, oh, thought Marsha. She walked quickly over to her mother and Wendy. "You're way too big," she said to Wendy.

"No! Ain't. Me ain't too big!" Wendy slammed her fist on the edge of the metal cart. She seemed oblivious to the pain but pleased by the rattly noise.

"Maybe you will fit," Kate said quickly. "Let's give it a try."

"She looks ridiculous," Marsha whispered. In her head she added "dumb, stupid, and retarded." Her mother awkwardly hoisted the eight-year-old into the cart's seat.

Wendy shoved her feet through the openings and slid down.

She smiled for just a moment, then her brow wrinkled. "Ow! Leg! Get out a here!"

Marsha and her mother each grasped one of Wendy's flailing arms and tried to pull her out. The cart reared up as they struggled, and Wendy shrieked, "Ow! Ow! Ow!"

Several shoppers turned to look while Marsha tried to avoid their stares.

Finally, Wendy was out and on her feet again.

Kate's face was flushed, and she sighed wearily before saying, "Okay. Now is that better, Wendy?"

The girl rubbed her legs and whimpered. She mumbled something that sounded like a curse word.

"I'm sorry you got hurt," Kate continued. "But Marsha was right. The cart is too small for you."

"No. Me too big." Wendy's tone was serious.

"She's not *too* injured," Marsha said to herself as Wendy dashed off down another aisle.

"Could you keep track of her for a sec', Honey? I've got a lot of things to find. I hate the way this store is organized. The one in Richville is so much better."

Marsha caught up with Wendy at the school supply section where she was squeezing a plastic bottle of white glue. Wendy peered intensely at the cap, waiting for something exciting to happen.

"May I see that?" Marsha asked tentatively. Yelling at Wendy didn't seem to work, so she tried a different approach.

"See?" Wendy held the bottle up and gave it another hard squeeze.

Marsha looked away and thought seriously about leaving the store, getting back in the car, and letting her mother handle whatever disaster was bound to happen.

She let her eyes wander over the shelves because she was afraid to look directly at Wendy. One whole section of a shelf was devoted to a display of crayons. Marsha picked out a box of sixteen.

"You like crayons, Wendy?"

"Got some. At school. Daddy give me some." She seemed to be losing interest in squeezing the bottle. Next she began to unscrew the cap. She grunted with concentration and effort.

"I'll bet Mommy'll buy you this really neat set of sixteen crayons to use at home," Marsha said.

Wendy looked up at Marsha, and her eyes narrowed.

"After you put the glue back, you can have the crayons. Just ask Mom nicely. Be sure to say 'Please', okay?" Marsha added.

Wendy frowned. She glanced down at the glue in her hand.

A bird in the hand is worth two (or sixteen) in the bush, Marsha thought with a glimmer of amusement.

"There you are," Kate said, coming around the end of the aisle. "I've been looking all over for you."

Not hard enough, Marsha thought.

Wendy tossed the glue back on the shelf and snatched the crayons from Marsha.

"Me wan' these!" she said belligerently.

"How'd I tell you to ask?" Marsha shook her head in disgust.

Suddenly a dramatic change came over the little girl. She smiled sweetly, and holding the crayon box above her head with both hands, she said, "Please?"

Kate grinned. "Sure. Why not? Marsha, is there anything else we need?"

"Did you get the hot dogs?" she asked because she couldn't see any in the jumble of groceries in the cart.

"Oh, I forgot. Would you go back and get a couple of packages? I'll get in line with Wendy. That'll save a little time."

Thankful for an excuse to get away from Wendy, Marsha went and found the hot dogs. She picked out ones made from turkey—five packages, because she'd seen how Wendy could devour hot dogs.

When she got back to the check-out line, she was surprised to see Wendy standing quietly next to Kate.

"See? Turkey franks," said Marsha. "I bet even Aunt Laura would approve. Do you think she'll come to visit soon?"

As soon as she asked the question, Marsha realized her mother would be upset. She knew how critical Aunt Laura could be and that this made her mother annoyed and resentful. Today, however, Marsha didn't care whether she was being mean to her mother.

She got us into this adoption mess, Marsha thought. Before Wendy came, everything was fine.

Kate plopped two bags of apples on the counter. "I hope your dear Aunt Laura doesn't come to visit. Not for a long, long time."

Marsha kept quiet while her mother paid for the groceries. As they started to leave the store, Wendy noticed the gum machines. Before she could begin to beg, Marsha quickly rummaged through a bag, located the crayons, and held them up.

With a cry of, "Gimme!" Wendy grabbed them. All the way to the car, she glared at Marsha and muttered, "Mine," every few steps.

After helping her mother put the groceries in the car trunk, Marsha climbed into the front seat. Kate seemed tired and distracted. She didn't tell Marsha to move in back with Wendy.

By the time they arrived home, Wendy had chewed up all her new crayons.

"Oh, for heaven's sake!" exclaimed Kate. "Why didn't you watch her, Marsha? You should have sat next to her. We should have left those stupid crayons in the bag. What a mess!"

Wendy grinned, exposing teeth flecked with various colored bits of crayon. A scrap of paper wrapping hung from her upper lip—green-yellow, it read.

Marsha watched her mother wipe some of the particles off Wendy's teeth. "I didn't know she'd do that, Kate. She's eight years old. Who'd expect her to eat crayons? Even Rosie's littlest sister knows you don't eat crayons!"

"Oh, hush, Marsha. And please quit that *Kate* business. You're just going to confuse Wendy." Her mother's voice had a brittle edge to it.

Fighting back tears, Marsha slammed the car door and started toward the house.

"Come back here!" her mother called. "I need help with these packages."

Marsha ran back, grabbed a bag, and hid her face behind it. As she walked quickly and blindly to the side door of the house, she tripped and almost fell.

9

February 8
Dear Diary,
Sometimes I can't remember what it was like before Wendy came to live with us. It seems so long ago!

I used to have my own room all to myself. Rosie could stay overnight on weekends. But now she hardly ever comes to visit. Sure, we see each other at school every day. But it isn't the same.

Sometimes I get the feeling she doesn't want to be my best friend anymore. It's partly because of Wendy. I found out Rosie told Mike about Wendy that first day. He asked where I was on the bus that morning, and she told him I had to ride to school with my new retarded foster sister. At least she didn't tell him my parents plan to adopt Wendy. I was mad at Rosie for about three days. Things have sort of gotten back to normal, but not quite.

I just wish Wendy could move into her own room! We have another bedroom, but it's been used for storage forever. Our attic is too hot in the summer and too cold in the winter for most stuff. One time we put our Christmas candles up in the attic, and the next year when we brought them down, they were all crazy-looking shapes. They'd melted during the summer.

Cleaning out that stupid storage room is going to take forever—which is why we haven't started on it yet. Maybe next summer. . . . . .

Anyhow, sharing my room with Wendy is awful! She takes ages to go to sleep. She keeps talking to me right up 'til the second the Sandman knocks her out. Not only is she a pest, but J.J. acts like she's his favorite person. And he's been my friend ever since I can remember. How can he do this to me?

Enough about Wendy! At school Mike still teases me. I don't know if I like him or not. Last summer I used to spy on his house from our woods. I'd get this tingly feeling whenever I'd see him all-of-a-sudden. Now, I don't know.

Rosie has a boyfriend! At least she says she does. His name is Butch, and he's in the other sixth grade class with Mike. He lives in town, and his big brother has a motorcycle. Rosie says she wants to ride that motorcycle. I don't know if she really likes Butch or his brother or maybe just his brother's motorcycle!

Rosie used to be my very, very best friend. But, like I said before, sometimes I feel like she wants things to change. But maybe it's just me. I don't feel so comfortable with her anymore. She's so different this year. When I go over to her house, she wants to fool with Violet's makeup or lie around and listen to tapes or watch stupid soap operas.

Mom just told me to turn off my light. One more thing—that social worker, Ms. Kerp, came to visit a couple of days ago. Mom freaked out getting the house clean. She never cleans unless somebody is coming, and then she goes crazy. With Wendy around making one mess after another, it's like a disaster area around here all the time.

I guess Ms. Kerp is okay, but she makes me feel uncomfortable. She tried to talk with Wendy. Guess who hid in my closet and wouldn't come out for anybody, even Dad. Mom was kind of upset. But Ms. Kerp said not to worry. She said Wendy was probably afraid she'd come to take her away. When she said that, I wanted to shout, "Well, take her!" But, of course, the old marshmallow kept her trap shut.

Since Wendy wouldn't come down, I ended up talking to Ms. Kerp-Burp. Funny thing, mostly she asked about me. How school is going, stuff like that. So I didn't get a chance to tell her about Wendy's screaming fits. She has one at least once a day! Mom calls them her "screamy-meanies."

I'm sleepy. Night-night.
Marsha

March 2

Dear Diary,

March came roaring in yesterday—rain and wind. So it's supposed to go out like a lamb. That's silly, but everybody says it. Even that retarded weatherman with the whiny voice on T.V.

I guess I shouldn't use <u>retarded</u> like that. But everybody does. Now that I have a real retarded kid living with me, I sort of jump inside when I hear somebody say it. They mean it like a joke or silly insult, but it still bothers me.

Tonight I tried to get J.J. to sleep in my bed. But he hopped back down and now he's with her— Wendy! I don't see how he can like her after what she did to him last week.

She's always doing something! I bet I can think of ten terrible things she's done in the past couple of weeks.

Here goes—

1. Fed all the toothpaste to the toilet (except what she ate herself)!

2. Gave J.J. a bath—and he still loves her!

3. Got a whole bunch of scratches on her hands, arms, and face—thanks to J.J.

4. Because of those scratches, her teacher stopped me in the hall to ask me what happened to Wendy. I felt like she thought I did it to the little creep!

5. Ate all the best cereals in just two days. Now all we have left is generic junk with names like Super Fiber Smacks and Wheat Wonderfuls.

6. Made Kate and David have some arguments about how to handle her. Dad thinks they should be gentle with her. Mom thinks they should be firm with her. I'm for Mom!

7. Interrupted at least fifty times whenever I tried to talk to Mom about something important.

8. Screamed into the other phone while I was talking to Rosie. She's done that every time I'm on the phone.

9. Lost 1 Barbie sundress, 2 earrings (not a pair), 5 single shoes, and the leg off my best Barbie, the one I call Laura. I wonder what Aunt Laura would do if she were missing a leg?

10. Ate the erasers off all my new Garfield pencils (except the two I took to school the day I got them).

11. Tore three pages out of a school library book—and Kate says I have to help pay for it because I left it lying around where Wendy could find it. How will I ever save money for my horse with Wendy here?

12. Made a fool of herself on the school bus— every day. She screams and cries sometimes. Or she giggles. And she swears, too!

13. Won't go near Butterscotch. She knows I want her to like him, I think. And she acts like the saddle is an electric chair.

See? That's Thirteen Terrible Things she's done. She's even worse than I thought! One thing is better. A little. She doesn't scream as loud or as often, at home. Or maybe I'm just getting used to the noise. She's talking better, too, but she still can't say my name!

Your friend,
Marsha

10

Marsha took another bite of her hot dog encased in a squishy roll and almost gagged.

"I'm sick of hot dogs," she said.

"Wendy likes them," Kate said in a flat, automatic tone of voice. She'd been giving the same answer to the same complaint for weeks.

"Wendy's been here for almost two months, Mom. Can't she adjust to real food?" Marsha imagined a plateful of lasagna or fried chicken. Even tuna casserole would have been a welcomed relief.

"Now, Marsha," David said calmly. "Wendy has so many adjustments to make. Let's not force strange food on her, too."

Wendy grinned around the hot dog she was jamming into her mouth. Marsha tried not to watch, but there was something fascinating about this kid's technique. She put such incredible amounts in her mouth; Marsha was certain one of these days she'd choke.

I wonder who'll jump up and pound her on the back or use the Heimlich maneuver to save her life, Marsha thought. Maybe no one. Maybe we'll all sit here and watch her turn red, then blue, and slide to the floor . . . Now I'm getting gruesome, like Rosie. We could use it for a Barbie story. Maybe Laura will choke. She's been eating too much to compensate for her lost leg.

"Wendy!" Kate said, interrupting Marsha's train of thought. "Let's eat slowly and chew the food."

Wendy nodded as she used all ten fingers to expertly poke the last three inches of her second hot dog into her wide open mouth.

Kate slammed her own fork down onto her plate.

"Stop that! Wendy, you just can't eat like that."

Yeah, Mom! thought Marsha.

She glanced at her father, who was watching Kate. He didn't interfere.

"Now, Wendy," Kate said gently. "If you want another hot dog, I'm going to cut it up in tiny pieces. You have to count to twenty between eating each piece. Do you want another hot dog?"

Wendy nodded vigorously. Then remembering the magic word, she said, "Please."

"Good." Kate sighed. "Now, what am I going to do with your hot dog?"

"Give me!" Wendy's grin was triumphant.

"Yes, but first I'm going to cut it up, remember?"

"Okay," replied Wendy. When her plate with its chopped contents was returned to her, she attacked the pieces with her fork.

"One at a time," David admonished. "Does she know what *one* means?" he asked Kate.

"Of course." Turning to Wendy, Kate added, "You're very good with numbers, right, Honey? Now, please count to twenty."

"One, two, three, four . . ." Wendy counted with her mouth wide open.

"She's never going to chew her food while she's counting," remarked Marsha.

"Can she really count all the way to twenty?" David asked.

"Yes," said Kate. "You can count all the way to fifty, can't you, Wendy? But Marsha's right. I'll count, Wendy, and you chew. With your mouth closed!"

As Wendy's hot dog eating continued with Kate counting loudly, Marsha found herself chewing in time to the beat. When the meal was finally over, she helped her mother clear the table. Wendy scooted off to the living room to watch television.

"I see we got another letter from Laura," said David. He was looking through the mail on the kitchen counter.

"Don't bother to read it," Kate said. "She just says the same old things."

"Don't let her get you down, Katie." His smile was sympathetic. He put his arm on her shoulder, and she turned to him.

Marsha leaned against the counter and purposefully looked out the window. She found it embarrassing when her parents acted affectionate.

"It's just that sometimes I get scared." Her mother was almost whispering, her face pressed against David's chest. "You know what I mean? I've always been able to dismiss the things she's told me—all that unsolicited advice. I know she resents the fact that you married me. I'm not good enough for her precious baby brother."

"Hush," David said gently. "Don't worry about that old bat. She's just never forgiven you for wanting to do the same things I love to do—teaching and living in the country. She's a frustrated old maid."

"Stop that, David! Now you sound like an ignorant male chauvinist."

Marsha wasn't sure whether her mother was kidding or getting angry.

"Besides, she's hardly an old maid!" Kate continued. "She's only two years older than you, and she has lots of male friends. I don't think marriage has ever been in her plans, but that's all irrelevant. The problem is, I feel as if, for once, her criticism makes some sense. And that's what scares me!"

"Forget it! Nothing Laura has ever said has made sense to me. She's been trying to boss me around since I was two years old."

Marsha scooped some leftovers into a dish for J.J. At least he still thinks hot dogs are a treat, she thought.

"Actually, I admire Laura," David said. "But she's got to realize that she's living her life the way she wants to, and we're living our lives the way we want to. It's as simple as that! I don't let her opinions or advice get to me."

Kate sniffed slightly and turned on the water to fill the sink. "That's fine for you to say. You grew up with her. I guess my skin isn't quite as thick as yours."

"Well, we're doing what we think is right for us. So what if we get scared sometimes. Life would be awfully dull without a few scary moments. We'd smother in boredom, right Marsha?" With that remark, her father winked at her.

Marsha's nod was cut short by a tremendous crash in the living room.

"Oh, no! What now?" cried Kate.

Marsha followed her parents into the living room. The lamp which usually sat on the end table next to the couch now lay in a shattered mess on the rug. Wendy was huddled in a small, sobbing ball beneath the dining room table.

"How'd that happen?" David asked. "We've only had that lamp since Christmas!"

Between sobs Wendy repeated, "J.J., J.J. . . ."

"Yeah, I bet," Marsha whispered to herself. "Blame it on the poor defenseless cat. You're not so stupid."

Wendy emerged from her hiding place slowly, her eyes wide as she stared at the broken pottery and shattered light bulb.

"J.J. on table . . ." she said haltingly. "I pick up. He hanged on thing. You know? Thing under lamp."

"The place mat? The place mat that I had under the lamp?" asked Kate.

Wendy nodded. A tiny smile pulled up the corners of her mouth. Marsha realized that the little girl was pleased that she'd been able to make Kate understand so quickly.

Kate gave Wendy a quick hug. "Okay, Honey. Thank goodness you didn't get hurt. Now you go upstairs and wash your face. We'll clean up this mess. You'd better leave Jumpin'

Jehosephat alone for awhile. He's probably pretty upset."

Wendy trotted off obediently.

"We should have been watching her," Kate muttered while she busied herself stacking the largest pieces of the lamp base. "The silly thing must have hit the wooden arm of the couch. That's why it broke. What a mess! Marsha, get the vacuum, okay?"

"I'll get a trash bag for the bigger hunks," David offered.

"If only someone had been watching her," Kate said again.

Noticing that her mother was close to tears, Marsha remembered that the lamp had been a gift from David. With a sigh, she dragged the vacuum cleaner from the closet and plugged it in.

Does Mom mean I should have been watching Wendy? Marsha wondered. I can't watch her all the time! And neither can you, Mom. She acts like a baby! She embarrasses me in front of my friends. You watch her! You wanted her!

Marsha's words echoed inside her head, but her mouth stayed grimly shut. She stood awkwardly, looking on as her parents worked together cleaning up the pieces of the broken lamp. Wendy came hesitantly back into the room and sidled up to Kate and David.

Marsha felt a distance between herself and the others. Her father glanced at her and mouthed above the roar of the vacuum, "It's okay."

Then he patted the top of Wendy's head, and she smiled up at him.

Suddenly Marsha felt as if she'd burst if she didn't get away from them all. Her emotions seemed jammed together inside her like toy snakes in a can. If she stood there another second, her mouth would pop open, and the snakes would come leaping out— screaming snakes, not funny ones.

Marsha turned away and walked stiffly to the kitchen, jerked her jacket off its hook, and marched outside. There she took two quick gasps of fresh air before chasing her shadow to the barn.

11

Within the quiet false twilight of the barn, Marsha's gasps turned to sobs. She climbed up into the hayloft quickly, frantically, not caring if she slipped and fell.

The rough edges of the bales scratched her knees through the worn fabric of her jeans. She scrambled to the highest place and flung herself down to cry.

Gradually she stopped. Rolling onto her back, she let the feelings of exhaustion and calm seep over her.

The space between Marsha and the ceiling was hollow. She knew if she stood and looked up, the sense of height and emptiness would make the backs of her knees tingle.

She sat up and wrapped her arms around her bent knees. The only sound she could hear was the comfortable coo of pigeons.

Going back to the house did not seem like an option.

Maybe I can move out here, she thought. I could put a mattress on the bales. It might get chilly, but the weather'll warm up soon. Then I wouldn't have to worry about Wendy.

Marsha pulled a thin blade of hay out of a bale and began to chew on it. Wendy . . . Wendy . . .

Why couldn't Wendy be like the character in the movie *Peter Pan?* That Wendy was going to grow up. This Wendy—the real one—was never going to grow up, at least not completely.

It's confusing, thought Marsha as she replaced the piece of hay with another. Wendy can't grow up; I can but don't want to.

By blinking one eye, and then the other, Marsha made a blue-grey pigeon appear to hop back and forth on a beam. She was beginning to feel restless and wondered what time it was. She guessed that there was still about an hour of daylight left—enough time to ride Butterscotch through the woods. It didn't matter to her today that he was too small. She was sure he wanted to get out of the pasture as much as she wanted to escape the house. No one would see them anyhow.

Collecting the bridle and a handful of oats, she went into the pasture.

"Hey! Butterscotch!" she called, then whistled the two-note call that was special for the pony. He came from behind a clump of spindly bare-branched trees and tossed his head at the scent of the oats.

When he started to eat from her palm, Marsha slid her free hand up over his nose. Then she expertly slipped the bit into his mouth while he was still munching. She pulled the pony's ears gently into place and arranged his forelock neatly.

"Sorry I tricked you, Old Boy. But, after all, I haven't ridden you in ages."

The pony gazed at her with his soft, brown eyes.

"Is that a forgiving look?" Marsha grinned and patted his fuzzy neck. Soon he'd be losing his long winter coat. It would come out in matted clumps—perfect for spring birds' nests. But now he looked like an overgrown and shaggy dog.

Mounting Butterscotch was a simple matter. Marsha hopped onto his back and collected the reins. A few years before she had needed a running start or a large rock.

Marsha opened the gate and shut it without dismounting. Butterscotch was excited and pranced jerkily. Marsha sat loosely, her legs hanging straight down, while calming the pony with her relaxed body.

They skirted the edge of the backyard and entered the woods which grew on either side of the creek. A thin path ran along roughly parallel to the lazy stream of water. Sometimes the path came within a foot of the creek, but most of the time it threaded along the top of the sloping bank. The sure-footed pony trotted quickly.

During the summer the leaves made a private world here in the woods. Now, in late March, it was easy to see ahead along the curving creek.

They were heading into the sun, so the tree trunks were lit from behind, edged in brightness. The creek flowed toward the road, and Marsha and Butterscotch followed it partway. Then they turned and slid down the steep slope into the creek and across it. As her pony trotted out of the shallow water, Marsha shortened her reins, leaned forward, and pressed her legs close to his sides.

Butterscotch broke into a gallop, all of his contained energy released in his mad dash. Marsha loved the speed and sense of strength beneath her, but the pony was so small, she felt unbalanced. She pulled him back to a walk, and, for one second, she was sure she'd fall off right over his head. By clamping her legs tightly and leaning back, she managed to stay seated.

Just ahead the woods ended and the long hill began. Butterscotch pranced and stretched out his neck, asking for more rein so he could run.

"I'm sorry, Butter Boy. We can't. It's not ours. Not anymore. Not like it was before." Marsha flipped a portion of the pony's mane to the other side of his neck and patted the warm, damp area. She leaned back lazily and stretched out her legs. There was no longer any path, and her feet brushed against the winter-dead undergrowth. She took a deep breath, trying to smell the promise of spring, but there was a sharp chill in the air that reminded her only of winter.

Butterscotch turned left on his own and dropped his head to find food. He stopped and yanked at a tuft of dried grass at the edge of the woods.

Marsha ignored him, although she was usually strict about keeping him from eating while she rode. She could see Mike's house and several development houses clearly from here. Last summer she had often lingered in this part of the woods, staring at his house, sometimes catching a glimpse of him in the yard.

She swung her legs along Butterscotch's sides. "I can hardly wait 'til a bunch of bratty kids move into those stupid houses," she told the pony. "Sure wish Dad would put up a fence, so they couldn't get into our woods. They're going to ruin everything."

In answer Butterscotch flicked back an ear but continued to munch.

"Go ahead. Be a little piggy. See if I care. We're going to sell you anyhow. Let somebody else work on your manners."

Marsha let the reins drop onto his withers and began to bite her thumbnail. Then she looked at it closely, sighed, and started to nibble on a fingernail.

Marsha shut her eyes. She felt her pony take a step forward. It was so peaceful here. She stopped chewing her nails and began to hum. There were no words to the tune that came out of nowhere into her head.

Suddenly she felt Butterscotch's head jerk up. She opened her eyes. There, almost directly in front of her, was Mike Adams.

12

"Hi," said Mike. He stood beside a large walnut tree, aimlessly swinging a twig.

Marsha stared at him.

"Hi," he repeated. He whacked the twig against the tree trunk, and it broke with a sharp snap.

"Hey! Watch out. You'll scare my pony," said Marsha. Then she added, "What're you doing in my woods, anyhow?"

"Geez! These woods sacred or something? You sure are acting mean for a marshmallow. I always come here." Mike stared back at Marsha and then took a step closer.

She felt strangely uncomfortable. These woods were hers, a private sanctuary. Having Mike here, instead of a distant figure in his yard, was wrong. Maybe not wrong, but different.

She looked at him carefully. He didn't seem at all like the boy she'd spied on last summer. That boy had not been real, more like an imaginary friend, someone special, just for her. And yet, this Mike wasn't acting like the one at school or on the bus. That boy was a tease and a show-off. If he had seen her riding her undersized pony, talking and singing to herself, he would have greeted her with some clever put-down instead of, "Hi."

Mike glanced down and poked the broken remnant of his twig at the bark of a sapling beside him.

"What do you mean," Marsha asked, "you *always* come here?"

He shrugged. Using the stick he flipped some soft, leafy soil onto the toe of one sneaker. "I come here lots."

"Yeah?" Marsha began to feel warm despite the late afternoon chill.

Mike stared intently at his feet. "I was here 'most every day last summer."

"I bet. How come I didn't see you?" Marsha knew she would never have challenged him at school. But here, in her own space, she could.

We're not the same here, either one of us, she realized suddenly.

Mike's dark eyes met hers, and he smiled slowly. "Maybe you didn't know where to look for me? I saw you. I like to climb trees."

Had he been watching her from a tree some of those times she'd hung around spying on his house? Marsha patted Butterscotch's neck self-consciously. She studied his mane and then pulled her fingers through it, yanking at a tangle.

Finally, she glanced at Mike. He was still looking at her. She felt her face growing hot, but she couldn't force her eyes away from his. Several seconds passed, then Mike grinned impishly. Marsha couldn't resist smiling back.

"What's so funny?" he asked. "I'm the one who should be laughing. At you! Riding that midget horse, and singin' to yourself."

Marsha shook her head, but the smile remained. "Remember Mrs. Wolf's class last year?" she asked. "You used to make me laugh just by giving me that silly grin of yours. Then she used to tell *me* to be quiet."

"I got in trouble all the time. That Wolf had it in for me," Mike said. "Still worth it, though. Being the troublemaker. School's too dull if you're a goody-goody all the time. Somebody has to liven things up."

"I suppose I'm the goody-goody. But you go too far, Mike, really."

"Oh, yeah? Then how come you never tell me to bug off? You're the easiest kid to tease. Easiest in that whole stinkin' school."

"What do you mean?"

"I mean you just sit and take it. You're like a soft, squishy marshmallow. What are you going to do next year in junior high with all those tough kids? Aren't you going to start to fight back?"

Marsha shrugged. "Probably not. I try just to ignore rude people."

Peeling the bark from his twig, Mike said, "I can't. Ignoring people isn't my style." He tossed the twig into the brambles. "In my other school, before we moved here, I was the littlest kid in my class—practically the whole school. I got in fights all the time. Real fights, not with words—with fists and feet and teeth."

"Sounds like fun," Marsha said sarcastically. "Did it work? Did they quit teasing you?"

Mike flashed a grin. "Nah. You kiddin'? I told you I was little." He held his hand out to knee height. "We're talkin' micro-mini. The kids got to tease me and beat up on me. It was the school sport. But I learned a lot. I know how to fight. Dirty, if I have to. But I don't. Not in this dumb school. I learned to dish out insults, too. Comes in handy. I know how to spot a kid's weak points. Best part is, I get other kids laughing. It's fun."

"Not for everybody," Marsha said quietly.

Mike didn't seem to hear her. "I like to get Rosie going. Almost anything I say will set her off. Once she gets started, I can just make a few faces, and the others keep right on laughing."

"Maybe you two should become a comedy team," Marsha said.

The sun dropped behind the hill, and a breeze began to rustle through the thin, bare tree branches. Marsha shivered unexpectedly.

"I gotta go," she said as she pulled up the hood of her jacket. "It's going to be dark soon. And I didn't tell my parents where I was going."

"Sure." Mike kicked at a tree trunk to loosen the dirt on his sneakers. "Your parents nice?" he asked abruptly.

"Yeah, I guess so."

"How come they want to have that little foster kid?"

"I don't know. It's kind of hard to understand. Even for me."

"My parents wouldn't do that—take in some kid they didn't know. Guess I'm enough of a troublemaker. My dad's always mad about something. When he's home. And when he's not, Mom's mad about that and takes it out on me. Guess that's why I come here. It's kind of peaceful."

"I know."

Darkness was gathering into shadows within the woods while the breeze stirred the tall, brittle grass in the field.

"Well, I'll see ya' around," said Mike as he took a few steps backwards.

Marsha turned Butterscotch toward home, looked back, and waved. Mike raised his hand, and although his face was lost in the shadows, she knew that he was smiling.

13

April 7
Dear Diary,
Yesterday was Rosie's birthday. She got lots of clothes and three pairs of pierced earrings. She's getting her ears pierced next weekend. Gross! I don't want anybody poking a needle through me. But the earrings are neat. Aunt Laura has pierced ears, and she's always wearing these gorgeous, dainty earrings.

Aunt Laura called a couple of days ago. I heard David talking to her. He sounded mad, but when he saw me, he must have guessed I was listening, so he changed the subject. I'm sure they were talking about Wendy.

That same night, while Wendy and I were watching T.V., I heard Kate and David talking in the kitchen. They weren't actually arguing, but they weren't actually kissing, either. It makes me feel real edgy when they have one of their discussions. I think about all the kids whose parents are divorced. Maybe those kids thought it'd never happen to them. What if Mom and Dad split up? Or what if they died? Or what if there was a nuclear war? Or the hole in the ozone layer opened up real wide?

I start with Wendy and end up with global disasters. I wonder if that's a bad omen?

Oh, I forgot. Butch (remember, he's Rosie's boyfriend) gave her a present at school. It's one of those thin chains with an itsy-bitsy heart attached. Rosie told me she loves the necklace, but she's sick of Butch. I told her she could always give it back, but she doesn't want to.

And my love life.?? I'm all mixed up about Mike. Mom would say I had a crush on him last summer, not that I've told her about him. But she does talk about that stuff. Like things she thinks I should know about growing up. Love and sex and responsibility. I don't like it when she gives me one of her little speeches. I don't feel ready to grow up!

Anyhow, about Mike. Ever since our talk in the woods, he's been acting different at school and on the bus. He still teases me, but he's not so mean. Or maybe I just don't mind so much. Sometimes he looks at me, and our eyes meet, and it's like we're talking, even though we're not.

Mike's been teasing Rosie a lot. She loves it.

Gives her a chance to mouth off at him. She probably likes hearing the other kids laugh as much as he does.

I still have six pages to read in my science book tonight. Ever since I got a C on a report (all Wendy's fault), I feel like I have to work extra hard in science.

Mrs. Swanson hung my last book report on the bulletin board. The book I read was <u>Peter Pan</u>. Maybe some kids thought that was funny 'cause they think it's a little kids' book. But it's not, really. I had never read the whole book before—the original. I loved it. But nowadays Wendy wouldn't have gone back to spring-clean for Peter. The story is kind of sad, too, at the end where it talks about people—and even Nana the dog—dying. And I feel sorry for Peter, too, because he never grows up. Anyhow, Mrs. Swanson put "Good Job" in red ink across the top of the report. Rosie called me a teacher's pet, but I don't think she meant it. And even if she did, I don't care.

Yours truly,
Marsha

May 12
Dear Diary,

It's been raining for days. I think toadstools are going to start growing on my rug. Yesterday Rosie came over, and we tried to play Barbies, but guess who kept butting in. We even went out to the barn, but she followed us.

Wendy has been living with us for four months. Soon the trial six months will be over.

Ms. Kerp visits us, and she's all right. Mom likes her a lot—says she's been very helpful during this adjustment period. Mom and Dad have joined some kind of support group for adoptive parents. Ms. Kerp told them about the group. When Ms. Kerp comes, at least Wendy doesn't hide from her anymore. In fact, she usually talks so much Ms. Kerp doesn't ask me any questions. Suits me fine.

David and Kate never talk about after the six months are up. Not in front of me. They never say anything about keeping Wendy or sending her back. It's like they just assume she's staying. But I keep thinking maybe it won't happen. Maybe Wendy won't stay. It's not like I want Wendy to be unhappy. But maybe she'd be better off with some other family—with some other sister she could get attached to. She always sits next to me on the couch when we watch T.V. And I've been reading stories to her— some of my old favorites, like *The Snowy Day* and lots of Dr. Seuss stuff and *Winnie-the-Pooh*. She loves to listen to me read. And she likes Mom and Dad and J.J., too. And she loves my Barbie dolls. She always wants to play with the one named Laura, the one with the missing leg. I've looked all over for that stupid leg! You'd think Wendy could find it since she's the one who yanked it off. She's real smart about finding other things—like all my Barbies even when I hide them. She leaves them on her bed with their hair all messed up and naked.

The only one in our family Wendy doesn't like is Butterscotch. And I can't think of any way to change her mind.

Last night Dad asked me what I want for my birthday next month. I said, "A horse." He looked real thoughtful and then said, "No. I think you should earn your horse. One gift horse, or pony, is enough for any kid. If you sell Butterscotch you'll have some money to put toward a new horse. Then you can earn the rest. We'll start paying you to baby-sit. Maybe you can do extra work in the garden this summer. John Bower might even pay you to help out with the chores over at their place. He was complaining to me the other day about how his own girls aren't much help."

Sure, I bet. If Rosie's dad won't pay her, why would he pay me? How'll I ever earn enough? And I'm not going to sell Butterscotch. No matter how much I want a horse. But sometimes I think it would be better for him, with a new home where he'd get some exercise. I haven't ridden him in weeks, and he's fat as the sow that Vi took to the fair a couple of years ago. I just have to think of some way to get Wendy to like him. Then I'll teach her to ride him.
Good-night.
Marsha

May 23
Dear Diary,
Just when I start to feel almost like Wendy's my sister, she does something awful, and I wind up hating her again. Rosie keeps telling me that it's okay to hate your sisters. But Wendy is worse than all of Rosie's combined.

Today I was so embarrassed! On the way to school on the bus, Wendy took her lunch out of her backpack and started digging through it. She always does that. I try to stop her, but she's too stubborn.

She took out her sandwich first. Then she shoved that back in and dragged out her dill pickle. I've told Mom not to give her those, but Mom just says, "She likes them. Don't get upset when she sniffs them." Well, that's fine for her to say. She's not riding the bus with the little sniffer. Sure enough, Wendy started putting that dumb pickle up to her nose. But it was wrapped in aluminum foil, so she had to unwrap it to get a really strong whiff.

Right away this bratty fifth grader, Jack Gernhart, saw her and said, "Look at the bloodhound!" Then he asked her real sweet and fake serious, "Does your pickle smell good?"

Wendy smiled and said very loud, "Yeah!"

She never should have answered that jerk. Rosie said, "Shut up, Jack. Leave her alone."

Of course, that got Mike into it. He said something like, "Rosie's jealous. I bet her Mommy didn't give her a smelly old pickle. What've you got, Bowwow Bower?"

Rosie laughed. "I'm buying my lunch."

Stupid Wendy didn't even know what was going on. "Here," she said. She threw her lunch at Mike. "Smell it!"

Mike made a big thing out of snuffling the bag. "Whew! Dirty socks!"

Then Jack grabbed Wendy's pickle and stuck the end up his nose. Everybody started screaming and laughing. The loudest was Wendy. "Pickle! Pickle! Pickle!" she kept yelling.

Ol' Cranstram slammed on the brakes, and the pickle fell out of Jack's nose, and everyone got real quiet. Except Wendy. She saw her precious pickle land on the floor, and she got mad. Then she went into one of her screamy-meany fits.

Cranstram came back and tried to calm her down. But she was all the way into her act by then. He finally gave up, and Wendy cried all the way to school. He wrote a cranky note to Mom and Dad. They didn't let me see it, but I think he said something about keeping retards off the bus. I told them exactly what happened. They've decided that David will drive Wendy to school mornings, and he'll try to drive us home some days, too. I hope that helps.

I do have some good news. Excellent news! I've thought of a plan to teach Wendy to ride Butterscotch. I'm going to give her my Laura Barbie doll. I haven't told Mom and Dad because they don't like bribes. I wish they did! Maybe I could get a new Barbie doll out of them for being so nice to Wendy. Actually, I'll be giving Wendy a reward, not a bribe, because she'll get the doll after she rides Butterscotch for the first time.

I have to stop writing. J.J. just jumped up on the bed with me. I'd better pet him before he deserts me again.

Yours,
Marsha

14

Rosie plopped onto a bale of straw in the passageway of the barn.

"Yuck! It's too hot for June." She shoved her thick, dark bangs off her forehead.

Marsha nodded. "Yeah. Feels like August."

"I bet my sister would take us to the pool in town," said Rosie. "Vi has been going every afternoon since it opened. She's in love with one of the lifeguards."

"But you promised you'd help me teach Wendy to ride. My parents are leaving in about half an hour."

"Oh, yeah." Rosie stifled a yawn. "Well, you know, you're the one keeps telling me how Wendy hates Butterscotch. Why not just forget the whole thing?"

Marsha took the bridle off its hook and ran her fingers along the smooth, flexible reins. She'd oiled all the leather the night before in preparation for this occasion. Shrugging her shoulders, she kept her back to Rosie.

Silence settled like dust in the old barn. There was no way Marsha could explain her feelings to her friend. In Rosie's mind, a pony was just a bicycle with hooves. Now this pony was an outgrown bike, ready to be traded in for a bigger, better model.

Sliding the bridle over her shoulder, Marsha began to nibble a thumbnail. She glanced at Rosie. Only last summer they'd played Indians in the pasture. Now Rosie was more interested in checking out lifeguards and experimenting with Violet's makeup. She didn't just act different; she looked different, too. The two girls had always been nearly the same height, but this past school year Rosie had grown and now stood half a head taller than Marsha. She walked and talked a lot like Violet and was starting to have a shape like her sister's. Under her thin jersey, Marsha could see the outline of a bra.

Suddenly Marsha couldn't think of a single good reason to have Rosie help out with Wendy. For a moment she watched her friend picking bits of straw off her dark shorts.

"I guess . . ." Marsha began slowly, then finished in a rush, "maybe it's better if I work with Wendy alone. She's still a little scared, and she'll probably do better without anybody else around. You could come back over tomorrow. Sunday afternoon's a good time to bake cookies, if it's not too hot."

"You're sure you don't need me?" Rosie hopped up and swung her long arms, creating a weak breeze in the still air. "If it means so much to you, teaching Wendy to ride, you know, I can stay and help. Honest. Don't be mad, Marsha."

"I'm not mad at you, Rosie. I hardly ever get mad. You know that!"

"Oh, don't give me that garbage. You do too get mad. Just 'cause you don't scream and throw things doesn't mean you're not mad. I can tell. You get real quiet and sort of squinty-eyed. You should try yelling, Marsha. It's good for your health."

"I'm not mad! See?" Marsha opened her eyes wide and stared at Rosie. "I'm not squinting. Please go swimming and call me tonight and tell me how many cute boys were at the pool."

"I bet Mike'll be there. Doesn't that make you want to come? I know you still like him. And he likes you. He's been acting almost nice to you lately."

Marsha shrugged. "I don't want to talk about it. Not now, Rosie. Besides, I have enough problems with Wendy. I hardly think about Mike anymore."

"Wendy. Wendy. She's just a stupid sister. Why are you killing yourself trying to teach her to ride? Your folks can take her shopping with them, and we can go off for some carefree swimming. Forget your troubles!"

"No. This is the perfect setup. I practically begged them to let me baby-sit. They'll be gone for hours. And I have Wendy all psyched up to ride. I've promised to give her my best Barbie, the one named Laura, right after her first lesson."

"That doll? The one with the missing leg? Boy, you know, you sure are generous!" Rosie giggled.

Marsha couldn't help grinning. "She still likes that doll best. And I've kept it hidden for a whole week, way in the back of the linen closet, so Wendy couldn't find it. Now she's really looking forward to getting it. And I've even managed to get her to keep her mouth shut about the whole thing. I bribed her to secrecy by promising her a new outfit for the doll."

"Smart! And sneaky. My sisters would never fall for it. I tell them to keep quiet, and they get out the megaphones. Guess there are some advantages to having a retarded sister." Rosie stuck out her lower lip and blew up at her bangs. "Too hot. Okay, you've convinced me. I'll go. I'll call you tonight." She got up and brushed off the seat of her shorts. As she stepped over the doorsill she added, "Good luck."

"Thanks. I'll need it."

15

After Marsha saddled and bridled Butterscotch and tied his lead rope to a sturdy fence post, she went back to the house. Her parents were still getting ready to leave. Kate couldn't find her hairbrush. Then David decided he needed to adjust the turn signals on the car.

Marsha sat at the kitchen table next to Wendy and wished they'd hurry. She felt sorry for Butterscotch standing out there alone, and with every minute that went by, she became more nervous about her whole plan. Wendy was eating popcorn and giving every other piece to J.J., who sniffed each white morsel disdainfully. He stuck around, however, hoping the menu would soon include tuna fish.

"Now remember, Marsha," her mother said, "the list of phone numbers where we'll be going is on the paper by the phone. Dr. Lawrence's number and the ambulance number are there, too.

You could call Rosie's parents in an emergency. I thought she was going to be staying here for a while."

"No, she decided to go swimming. Don't worry, Mom. Wendy and I will do fine. Right, Wendy?"

Acting as if she hadn't heard, Wendy dropped two bits of popcorn on the floor. She cocked her head as she watched J.J. halfheartedly bat at them.

David called from the driveway, "Okay, signals are working fine. Let's go, Katie!"

"Bye, girls," Kate said. "Do behave. We should be back around one o'clock. There's tuna in the cupboard for lunch. You can make sandwiches. There's soup, too. I think chicken noodle, or vegetable. Let me check . . ."

The car horn honked twice.

Kate slammed shut the cupboard door. "You'll do fine." She sounded as if she were trying to convince herself.

"Have fun, Mom," Marsha said, as her mother gave her a quick hug.

"Fun? We're just buying a new lamp and some things to repair fences."

"And going out to lunch," Marsha reminded her.

Her mother's smile was brief and anxious. "You're right, Honey. We'll have fun."

By the time Marsha waved good-bye to the tail end of the car, the kitchen floor was littered with popcorn.

"Come on, Wendy. Help me clean up." Marsha pulled the broom out of the closet and looked for the dustpan. It was never on its designated nail on the back of the door.

"No!" Wendy suddenly and loudly announced.

Oh, wonderful! Marsha thought as she glanced at the stubborn-faced little girl. I can't let her know that when she gets that look, I get a stomachache! I've only baby-sat when she's been in bed asleep. This could be a whole new experience, Marsha told herself while she fought a rising sense of panic.

"Come on, Wendy. Mom and Dad expect us to act like big kids. We can't leave this popcorn all over the place. You go look for the dustpan, please. Maybe it's upstairs."

Wendy still looked uncooperative. "Popcorn for her," she said belligerently.

"Who? Oh, J.J. *Her* is a *him*. You know that. Anyhow, you can see he doesn't like it. We'll give him some tuna at lunchtime."

"I want hot dog!" Wendy's sudden grin was broad and self-assured.

Marsha knew better than to say no to hot dogs. "We'll see. Now, please get the dustpan."

Shuffling her feet through the popcorn, Wendy left the kitchen.

She'd better hurry, thought Marsha. I want to have plenty of time for her first riding lesson before Mom and Dad get back.

She swept the popcorn into a fluffy mound in the middle of the floor. "Wendy!" No answer. The clock on the wall above the stove ticked loudly. Staring at it, Marsha tried to make sense of the hands and numbers while all her attention was focused on listening for Wendy. It was almost eleven o'clock.

"Wendy!"

J.J. came back into the room, eyed the pile of popcorn, and pounced, scattering it across the floor. Marsha gave him a gentle shove with the broom. Then she stopped and listened.

Muttering to herself, she ran upstairs.

"Wendy! Where you?" Marsha checked the bathroom first. She yanked aside the shower curtain and looked in the tub. Next she glanced in her parents' bedroom, then the storage room—everything in there except Wendy.

The door to Marsha's bedroom was open, and she stepped inside quickly. Wendy looked up, a guilty little grin on her face. She had dumped Marsha's Barbie doll bag upside down on her own unmade bed—Barbie dresses and shoes, earrings and boots, all in a tangled heap.

"Where pretty dolly?" Wendy's question was almost a whisper.

Marsha unclenched her fists. "You'll see her soon. I hope! Come on, put that stuff away. Now we have two messes to clean up."

"I wan' pink 'n' pretty dolly," Wendy whined, and her eyes filled with tears.

Oh, no, Marsha's thoughts were darting around inside her head. If she throws a screamy-meany, I don't know what I'll do.

"Okay, Wendy," she said carefully, trying to keep her voice calm. "Don't worry. I'll find dolly. I'm going to give it to you, remember? I promised."

"Where? Where dolly?" Wendy's voice grew louder and more demanding.

"I don't know," Marsha lied, "but I'll find her soon. Come with me. Let's hurry up and get everything done, so I can find Laura for you."

"Who that?" Wendy's eyes narrowed with suspicion.

"Oh, for Pete's sake, Wendy! Laura is the doll you want. That's her name. You can call her whatever you want after I give her to you. But first we have some things to do, okay?"

Wendy sat motionless, her eyes on Marsha's face. Then abruptly she began jamming the Barbie dolls and accessories back into the bag.

Marsha took a deep breath, cautiously relieved. Apparently, Wendy had decided to cooperate, at least for the moment.

They managed to get the popcorn cleaned up without the dustpan. Wendy popped more than one piece into her mouth, but Marsha pretended not to notice.

The air outside was even stickier and hotter than before, but Marsha wanted to keep Wendy's mind off the upcoming riding session.

"I'll race you to the tree beside the barn, Wendy!"

They both ran. Wendy with a pell-mell, almost tripping gait, and Marsha with an exaggerated lope, so that she could insure that the younger girl would win.

Wendy clapped ecstatically when she reached the tree first.

Marsha grabbed her hand, shook it, and then held on as she led her toward the pony. "Come on. Let's go see what Butterscotch is doing. Do you know why he's called Butterscotch? Well, he's the color of butterscotch candy, and he's just as sweet."

Butterscotch raised his head as he saw the girls. He whinnied softly, expectantly, as his ears pricked forward. Where's my treat for waiting here so long? his expression said.

Marsha grinned at him, but Wendy hung back. "Don't be afraid," Marsha reassured her. "See that thing on his back? That's called the saddle. It's just like a neat, little chair. See? It even has cute footrests called stirrups."

Nodding hesitantly, Wendy kept her eyes on the pony's head.

"You wait right here," Marsha said. "I'm going to lead him up and down and you'll see how tame he is—just like a puppy or a kitten. He's like a big J.J." She climbed over the fence and untied the pony. After walking him around the barnyard once, she checked the girth and tightened it again. Butterscotch was unusually placid in the midday heat. His pale golden tail switched constantly to ward off flies.

Marsha's face felt hot and damp. She had to make an effort to hold her smile, or it would melt away. "Nice, Butter. See? Isn't he sweet?"

Wendy had pulled a strand of hair partway over her face and was holding it with her fingers while she sucked her thumb.

For a moment Marsha felt guilty. She'd never seen Wendy look so pathetic. Even when they'd first met her, she hadn't sucked her thumb. "Just think," Marsha said as she stopped Butterscotch right in front of the younger girl. "After you sit in the saddle for a couple of minutes, I'll find that Barbie doll for you. She'll be yours forever. Okay?"

"Okay," Wendy mumbled around her thumb.

"Can you climb over the fence? I bet you can. You're a big girl, right?"

Wendy stared at the fence, and Marsha guessed she was remembering how she'd fallen off it during her first encounter with the pony.

"Come on. You can do it!" Marsha almost shouted in an attempt to be encouraging.

Suddenly Wendy scrambled over the fence more quickly than Marsha had thought possible. She landed with a thud next to Butterscotch. He flicked an ear back but otherwise acted unconcerned.

Now comes the hard part, Marsha thought. This is when

Rosie would have come in handy. She could've held Butter's head while I got Wendy into the saddle. I'll just have to tie him up real short. That'll work if he doesn't swing around and lean against the fence.

He didn't. In a moment Wendy was slumped on his back, clinging to the saddle horn. She looked frightened and trapped.

"Get down," Wendy whispered.

"Not yet," Marsha said, forcing a positive, cheerful tone into her voice. "We're almost done. I'm just going to lead Butterscotch a few steps. You hold on nice and tight. That's the way!"

Marsha untied the pony and led him along the fence. She kept her head turned so she could watch Wendy. Slowly, step by step, they moved. Marsha began to relax. She flashed a grin at Wendy, but the little girl's mouth was set in a glum, straight line.

"Just a few more steps. You're doing great! Wait 'til Mom and Dad hear about this!"

Marsha turned Butterscotch away from the fence to head back toward their starting point. There was no reason to overdo it on the first day. She kept her eye on Wendy and noticed immediately when she started to slide sideways. Marsha grabbed Wendy's leg with one hand as she clung to the lead rope with the other. She walked backwards several steps, hanging onto Wendy's leg to steady her. Wendy's face looked pinched and frightened.

Suddenly Marsha tripped, stumbled, and fell down! The bucket she'd used earlier that day to lure Butterscotch with oats clattered and rolled away. The pony jumped forward, and the rope jerked from Marsha's hand as he broke into a trot. Like a confused whip, the lead rope flapped between his legs. He swerved and trotted faster, heading away from the barn.

Marsha scrambled to her feet and dashed after him, yelling, "Hang on, Wendy! Whoa!" The pony turned toward the trees at the other end of the pasture.

Bouncing wildly in the saddle, Wendy's feet bobbed out of the stirrups. She slipped precariously to the left, and her shrieks sent the pony into a canter.

It all happened quickly, although to Marsha, whose mind was recording it like a motion picture, it seemed elongated, endless. As if in slow motion, she could see Wendy's white-blond hair waving up and down, her legs flapping against the pony's sides, her body tipping, pitching over.

Suddenly she fell off.

When Wendy hit the ground, the camera in Marsha's head stopped rolling. A still shot—the small body, motionless on the trampled earth.

"Wendy!"

16

"Wendy! Are you okay?" The words were a high squeal, coming from Marsha's tight throat and dry mouth. "Answer me!"

Wendy sat up slowly, shaking her head in bewilderment. Marsha reached her and knelt, touching her arms and legs tentatively.

With an angry grunt, Wendy staggered to her feet. She turned dark eyes on Marsha and glared. "Stupid pony! I hate it!" She rubbed her face with her dirty hands, smearing tears and grime on her flushed cheeks, then held up her elbow to show an angry brush burn. "Ow! Ow! Ow!" she howled when she noticed the bloody scratches.

Marsha took a shaky but thankful breath. It could have been a lot worse. If Wendy's foot had slipped through the stirrup, she'd have been dragged, or Butterscotch could have stepped on her. Marsha shut out those thoughts. She reached over and attempted to brush the bits of grass and soil off Wendy's jeans.

Wendy jumped out of reach and screeched, "You mean, Marda! You made me ride stupid pony. Dumb! Stupid! Retard pony! Retard Marda!"

Marsha felt as if a fistful of gritty sand had hit her in the face. The truth stung. She swallowed hard and managed to say, "I'm sorry, Wendy." Gently, she took Wendy's sticky, hot hand.

"I ain't gettin' on again. No more! You learn somebody else. Not me! No way!" Wendy shook her head and wiped her nose on the back of her free hand.

"It's okay now," Marsha said, as she hugged the snuffling girl. "I'm really sorry. I shouldn't have made you ride Butterscotch. I was being stupid. Come on. Come sit down over here while I catch him. He'll step on a rein or trip over his rope for sure, if I don't hurry up."

After Marsha had removed Butterscotch's saddle and bridle, she took Wendy inside the house and washed and bandaged her injuries.

"I get dolly? Now?" Wendy asked hesitantly as she patted the thick wad of gauze and tape on her elbow.

"Sure thing." Marsha dashed upstairs and retrieved the Barbie from behind a stack of towels in the closet. She presented it to Wendy with a grin.

It felt to Marsha as if they'd passed through a storm together. Now it was over. Wendy's shy smile, as she cradled her new one-legged Barbie, was like a glimpse of sunshine.

"Read me story, Marda, please?"

"Okay, but aren't you hungry? I was just going to make you and me some lunch."

"Can I help?" Wendy asked.

"Sure!"

Wendy propped her Barbie doll against the flour canister. "So she watch us," Wendy said.

The two girls mixed the tuna with lots of mayonnaise and made fat sandwiches that oozed when they bit into them. Wendy never mentioned hot dogs. She ate two sandwiches and four pickles, and she only sniffed her pickles once or twice.

J.J. sat next to Wendy's chair, enjoying the globs of tuna filling that slipped out of her sandwich and onto the floor. When they'd finished eating, they did the dishes together. Wendy liked drying the silverware and putting it away in its special compartments in the drawer.

"Now I get book. Read to you," Wendy said.

"You mean I'll read to you," Marsha corrected her.

Wendy shook her head stubbornly and ran off. When she returned with an easy-to-read book, she surprised Marsha by reading page after page. The words came out haltingly and hardly above a whisper, but most of them were correct. Marsha put her arm around Wendy's shoulder, and despite the heat, they sat close together.

"What word that?" asked Wendy.

"Happy."

"Okay, *happy!*" Wendy glanced up and grinned.

When Kate and David arrived home Marsha was prepared to tell them what had happened—about the riding lesson and Wendy falling off, but mostly about how she felt differently toward her sister. Before she had a chance to say a word, Wendy greeted them.

"See owie? I got hurt," Wendy said, shoving her bandaged arm under David's nose.

"Marsha, what happened?" asked Kate as she came into the kitchen where the girls were peeking into a large bag which David had set on the table.

"It's a lamp," he told them. "Now, what happened?"

"Nothing . . ." Marsha began.

"I fell off stupid pony!" yelled Wendy.

Immediately, both parents turned toward Marsha. She felt a change of mood in the air. Tension and anger now hung in the space between her and them.

"It was an accident," she said quickly.

"An accident? How'd she get up on Butterscotch in the first place?" Kate's pale face was strained.

Wendy grabbed David's hand. "She make me. Marda make me ride retard pony." The hurt and fear came back into her voice.

Her eyes began to fill up with tears at the thought of the injustice and injury. "Marda give me Barbie doll. You wanna see dolly? She pretty."

"Marsha!" her mother said accusingly. She sounded disappointed as she continued, "We left you in charge to take care of Wendy."

Wendy forgot about the doll and began to cry in earnest. Still clutching David's hand, she leaned against Kate, sobbing dramatically.

An invisible wall sprang up, separating Marsha from the tight group formed by her parents and Wendy.

"You promised her a doll if she'd ride Butterscotch?" her father asked, his expression concerned and puzzled.

Marsha barely nodded.

"But why?" asked Kate. "You knew she was scared stiff of the pony."

Suddenly Marsha wanted to break that wall down—smash it with sharp words. She wanted to force her parents to be sorry for getting Wendy, for changing her life, and for making her feel so alone and helpless.

"I wanted Wendy to stop being scared of Butterscotch. I wanted her to learn to ride him. Then you wouldn't expect me to sell him. If Wendy could learn to ride him, I figured we'd keep him." Marsha's lower lip began to quiver, but she went on. "I just . . . I just wanted her to ride like a real sister. I wanted her to be normal!"

"Marsha, Honey . . ." her mother began. She took a step forward, reaching out to take Marsha in her arms. But Marsha stepped back. She had to say it all.

"It's not the same around here. You know it! It's all different since she came. She can't do anything right. She . . . she can't even say my name!"

Through a blur of tears, Marsha could see Wendy's injured expression. Her parents' faces had the same look. She couldn't stand seeing them a minute longer.

"Marsha," said Kate. "We didn't know . . . we don't . . . I mean . . ."

Marsha just shook her head. She couldn't help her mother

or herself. As she pushed past them to the door, she heard her father say quietly, "Let her go, Katie."

Across the yard she ran, past the barn, and over the fence. Butterscotch watched her trot through the pasture.

She was still running when the woods closed in. Despite the dense shade, there was no relief from the pressing afternoon heat.

Her feet skidded as she rushed to the edge of the creek. There she crouched and stared at the reflection of tree tops' and patches of sky. Shifting her focus, she looked beneath the surface to the muddy, pebbly bottom where a minnow flashed here, now there.

For months she had wanted to tell her parents how she felt.

I did it, she thought. But instead of triumph she felt confusion and anger.

Then she heard voices. They were loud and self-assured, coming closer. Her first impulse was to run away, to hide and watch. Instead, she forced herself to remain. She had every right to be here, in her own family's woods.

Three children appeared around the bend in the creek. They were all laughing and talking as they bobbed along the edge of the water, using the large, nearly flat shale stones to keep their sneakers from getting drenched.

Mike was one of them. He was in the lead with a long stick in his hand. He poked at the smaller rocks, flipping them over to expose the salamanders and worms.

"Hey!" he called. "Hi, Marsha." He looked directly at her, the beginning of a grin on his face. "No pony today?"

She shook her head and stood up. "And you're not spying from trees."

"Nope! Swinging from them. You want to try it?" he offered without bothering to introduce his companions.

"What? Like from a vine or something?" Marsha asked.

"A rope. It's right behind you a little ways. Where the bank's real steep. Come on. I'll show you."

The two other children came closer. One was a girl about Marsha's age. The boy looked younger.

"You have your own pony?" asked the girl.

Marsha nodded.

"My name's Dorey. I wish we could have a pony, don't you, Bobby?"

Her brother was busy trying to catch minnows. "Hey, Mike. I bet we could get us a whole mess of salamanders and little fish and stuff and keep 'em in jars. Maybe we could sell 'em or something."

"Naw," Mike answered quickly. He didn't look toward Marsha, yet somehow she felt he was protecting the woods for her. "Nobody would want to buy those silly things."

"Bobby, wouldn't it be fun to have a pony?" persisted his sister.

He just shrugged.

"Come on," said Mike. "Let's go try the swing."

The three children scampered up the bank and raced along the path. Marsha followed slowly along the edge of the creek.

When she reached the rope swing, Mike was already sailing high out over the creek. He had selected the perfect spot. The rope was tied to a strong branch that grew out over the stream. The tree itself was at the top of the steepest part of the bank, where the drop was like a cliff.

Mike grinned at her and winked, then he dropped back onto the bank.

"You're next, Bobby," Dorey told him. "Hurry up! I want my turn."

Marsha climbed to the top of the bank and sat down just as Bobby leaped off. He yelled and laughed, then landed and took off again.

"Get off! Show off!" his sister screamed at him.

Finally he dropped to the ground. "Awesome!" he exclaimed as he passed the rope to Dorey.

Dorey swung out without hesitation. Her legs were wrapped around the rope, but they slipped downward with her hands. She took one swing out and back to the bank just as she lost her grip. "That's hard!" she gasped. "I almost fell!"

"Come on, Marsha! Your turn. Don't be a marshmallow!" Mike stood with his legs apart, balancing on the slope. He held the end of the rope toward Marsha. The look in his eye was a challenge.

"What's with this kid?" Dorey laughed. "Does he have a nickname for everybody? He's already calling me Dopey Dorey, and we just moved in yesterday."

"You're in a development house." Marsha wasn't asking. She'd already guessed. She took the rope from Mike. The coarse hemp pricked her fingers. As she positioned her hands high up, she listened to Dorey's chatter.

"I love our new house. We used to live in this teeny, tiny apartment. Now I got my own room. Do you live around here?"

Marsha nodded.

"This woods is her property," said Mike.

Marsha took a quick, deep breath. She ran a few racing steps and leaped—far, far out. Her legs twined around the rope. The air flew past. She was at the end of a giant pendulum, rushing below and through the speckles of light and shadow, above the earth and water—suspended, moving, strong. Then the rope swung back, and she landed.

Dorey clapped and yelled, "Wheeee! You went farther than the guys!"

"I'm next," Mike said. "Watch this!"

They all kept swinging, taking turns until their faces dripped with sweat. They climbed down to the creek and splashed water on themselves and each other. Finally, Dorey told Bobby that they had to go home to help finish unpacking.

"Okay, Miss Mommy," he said sarcastically.

"See you around, Marsha. You in sixth grade, or what?" Dorey asked as she tried to brush mud off her light green shorts.

"Yeah. Mike and I are both in sixth."

"Me, too. But not for long. What do we have—less than two weeks of school left? Anyhow, I'll see you there. Bring your pony over to my house sometime. My little sister is horse crazy. She's only four. She's just ridden ponies at fairs and stuff like that."

"Sure, I'll see you in school on Monday," Marsha said.

Mike was hunched next to the stream, skipping pebbles across the narrow span of water. Bobby watched with admiration.

"Could you teach me how to do that?" he asked.

Mike shrugged. "Takes talent."

"Let's go. Mom'll be mad if we don't get home soon," said Dorey.

"You coming, too, Mike?" asked the younger boy.

"Sure," he said as he got to his feet. "So long, Marsha."

Something nagged at the back of Marsha's mind as she trudged up the hill toward home—something behind the images of Mike swinging and the remembered sounds of easy laughter. Suddenly she knew what it was. Hearing Dorey mention her little sister must have reminded Marsha of Wendy's angry comment. It was what Wendy had said when she fell off Butterscotch.

"You learn somebody else!"

"Learn somebody else . . ." Marsha murmured. "I will! That's exactly what I'll do."

17

June 3
Dear Diary,
Yesterday I tried to teach Wendy to ride. I didn't. She fell off, and later, when I was feeling pretty good about her, Mom and Dad came home and got mad at me. And then I told them off—really!

I told them how I've felt about Wendy from the beginning. The funny thing is, I don't hate her anymore. Not really. So I'm all mixed up.

Then last night Mom and Dad called me back downstairs after Wendy went to sleep. I knew something strange was going on because we had cocoa. It was too hot for cocoa.

Kate talked first. I can't remember exactly what she said. But I knew she was upset, even though she had this very quiet, reasonable voice. She said that what I'd told them made them realize they hadn't been including me enough in making decisions. Or something like that. She said they were sad to hear I felt that way about Wendy, but glad I'd told them.

I just sat there looking at my cocoa. No marshmallow. I kept wishing I had about five marshmallows. I wondered how many would fit in the cup before the liquid would come over the top—or maybe they'd just float above each other. I could just imagine these marshmallows piling up, and I'd have to hold them down with my spoon.

Then David asked if I was listening and told me to pay attention. He started telling me about this long talk he and Mom had. They want to keep Wendy. But they want me to be honest about my feelings. I didn't say a word.

So Kate began to talk again. She said that the trial six months were almost up and that if I feel that living with Wendy is impossible, I should let them know within the next ten days. Ms. Kerp will be coming to visit, and they'd want to tell her.

I asked, "If I say I don't want Wendy to be my sister, does that mean she has to leave?"

They both looked at me with these weird, puzzled expressions. I could almost hear them thinking, where did we get this monster?

Anyhow, Mom's face was getting all mushy-looking, and I was afraid she was going to cry. Dad said, "We want you to think about this very carefully,

Marsha. The final decision about adopting Wendy is up to your mother and me, but we want to hear how you feel. That's very important to us. We'll think seriously about your feelings when making our decision."

Then Mom said something that really surprised me. She said maybe Laura was right all along. Taking care of Wendy, living with a retarded child day in and day out is a lot different from just teaching kids like her. And that getting Wendy had been hard on all of us, especially because she wasn't a baby. Adopting any older child can be difficult, Mom said.

I don't know why they didn't think of that before!

After they quit talking, we all had some store-bought chocolate chip cookies. They weren't as good as the ones Mom makes. It was kind of nice, sitting there, just the three of us. I dunked my cookies, and Mom didn't tell me to stop. Funny, though. It wasn't really like old times because in a way we seemed closer, more like a family. And all the time I kept thinking about Wendy asleep upstairs and how much she likes chocolate chip cookies— almost as much as hot dogs.

So now my parents are waiting to hear what I have to say. And I don't want to say anything! Today Mom looked at me kind of funny a couple times, like she might be reading my mind. But she didn't ask me a thing.

Good-night,
Marsha

June 4
Dear Diary,
I've thought of a way to keep Butterscotch and earn
some money towards a new horse! I'm going to teach
little kids to ride. That way I'll get cash, and he'll
get exercise. I have to give Wendy some credit for this
idea. She told me to "Learn somebody else!"

Rosie says her mom wants Lily and Ivy to take
lessons—says they need something to keep them out
of her hair during summer vacation. I've told some
other kids at school about my idea, and a lot of them
have younger brothers and sisters. At least four kids
asked me for more information to show their parents.
So I have to write all the stuff down about
Butterscotch and how much I'll charge and when I'll
be giving lessons.

I bet there will be more small kids moving into
the development soon. There's already Dorey's sister.
I thought I'd hate anybody who came to live there.
But Dorey's nice enough. Rosie likes her, too.

Only a little over one week of school left! Then
in three days it'll be my birthday. Twelve! One more
year and I'll be a real teenager.

Good-night,
Marsha

June 7
Dear Diary,
I'm so tired. I need eye props. But Wendy is wide
awake singing to her stupid Barbie doll. Since she's
got a voice like J.J.'s when his tail gets shut in a
door, I can't go to sleep. So I might as well write.

Day before yesterday Mrs. Swanson, my teacher, told me that Mrs. Fisher, Wendy's teacher, wanted to talk to me. I thought, oh, no! What now! I went down the hall with my heart really thumping. I was sort of scared and mad, too. Why didn't Mrs. Fisher talk to Mom and Dad? Wendy's not my kid!

When I got to Wendy's room, her teacher was real nice. She told me her class was writing stories, and she needed some extra help. Mrs. Swanson had recommended me because I have good grades in English.

So it didn't have anything to do with Wendy!

That afternoon I got excused from gym class and went to Wendy's classroom. It was fun. I had to take dictation from the kids. They had some wild stories! And I learned one thing. The kids in that class are different. I mean from each other. I guess I used to think all retarded people were alike. But they aren't. Each one is special.

Like Wendy.

Tomorrow I'm going to make an information sheet about my riding lessons. It'll be a flyer with a picture and everything. Dad said he'd stop at the library and run off a bunch of copies for me. I'm going to ask Wendy to help me color them. She's good at coloring.

I still haven't said anything else to Mom and Dad about Wendy. I know that they're waiting. But I don't know what to say! Dad told me to think carefully—I'm thinking!

Guess what! Wendy's asleep!

Night-night,
Marsha

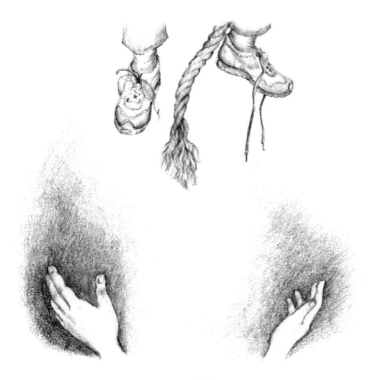

18

Wendy hopped off the bus first. "Bye-bye, Ol' Cranstram. Have nice summer!" she called.

Marsha peeked at the driver's face as she passed him, and she thought she saw the corners of his mouth give a reluctant twitch upward. Rosie and Lily filed off behind Marsha.

"Can you guys come over?" Lily asked above the grumble of the departing bus. Wendy looked at Marsha expectantly.

Marsha shook her head. "Not right now. Mom and Dad won't be home for a while. I'm going to make us lunch. Then we're going over to the development to pass out my flyers for pony riding lessons."

"Can't Wendy come over later?" Lily persisted. "I want her to see our baby kittens. And you haven't given me a flyer yet, and you promised you would, Marsha."

"Yeah, I forgot. Okay, we'll come over as soon as my parents get home."

"Wait'll you see the kittens," Lily said. "They're so tiny! Their eyes aren't even open yet." She squeezed her own eyes shut for emphasis.

Rosie glared at her. "The way you were picking them up and fussing over them, that momma cat has probably hidden them someplace by now."

"No, she didn't! She wouldn't! Her name's Princess, and she knows me. She likes me to pet her babies."

Rosie shrugged. "Come on, pest. I'm hungry. See you later, Marsha. By the way, what do you want for your birthday?"

"She want horse," piped up Wendy.

"I know that. But I can't get her a horse. What else? Hey, you want me to get you some earrings? Then your mom would have to let you get 'em pierced."

"No thanks. Really. I love your earrings, but not for me. Get me anything. I need socks."

"Need?" Rosie laughed. "Need socks! Marsha, you are impossible. With your imagination you should be able to come up with something better than socks. Gads!"

"Okay . . . Okay. How about a diary?"

"That's more like it. But I thought you already had one."

"It's almost full."

"Really?" Rosie's expression brightened. "You have to let me read it."

"Maybe—someday," Marsha said in a teasing tone. She did regret mentioning her diary. Now she'd have to put up with Rosie's pestering to read it.

"I know!" Lily shouted. "Let's give her a kitten."

"Oh, kitten." Wendy's brown eyes grew rounder at the thought.

"They're too little to leave their mother now. Marsha's birthday is in a couple of days," said Rosie. "I'll think of something. It'll be a surprise."

"Come on, Wendy. I think Mom bought some hot dogs for lunch."

On the way up the long driveway, Marsha took off her jacket. It had rained for two days, and early that morning the air had been cool. Now it was bright and clear. All the leaves looked crisp, like lettuce that had been soaked in icy water. It was a perfect day to go riding.

When I get my horse, Marsha thought, I'll ride all over on days like this.

"Ouch!" she yelped. "Wendy, watch where you're going."

"Okay," Wendy muttered as she lurched past with a large bulging paper bag under each arm.

"What've you got there?" Marsha asked.

"Stuff. Sweaters, my paints, my crayons, lots and lots and lots of papers, my sneakers . . ."

"Here, let me help. Give me one bag. You should have been bringing this junk home all week, instead of waiting for the last day."

Wendy nodded vaguely, a dreamy look on her face. "Kitties are nice," she announced a moment later.

She wants a kitten, Marsha thought. Well, maybe . . . Her birthday's in August. I bet Mom and Dad would say yes, and the kitten'll be just about the right age. I'll have to ask.

Then Marsha remembered. The social worker would be coming to visit the day after her twelfth birthday. If she told her parents that she didn't want Wendy to stay, and they told Ms. Kerp, then maybe Wendy would be gone by August.

Marsha scooped up those thoughts and dumped them in the back of her mind. It was too nice a day to be thinking about anything serious.

After lunch, Marsha brought out the stack of twenty flyers. Over the past few days Wendy had worked hard coloring each one. Marsha nodded with approval as she checked over the sheets.

"See?" Wendy asked with a broad grin. "I only out of lines here and here . . . and here."

"They look fine. Great! Now let's go give them out."

At the pasture fence they stopped. Marsha whistled for Butterscotch and rewarded him for his prompt response with a juicy apple. Wendy hung back, her eyes wide and fearful.

"Stupid pony," she mumbled.

When they stepped into the woods, Wendy's fear was gone.

She raced up and down the muddy slope next to the rain-swollen creek—slipping and sliding and laughing. She was like a baby bear coming out of his winter of hibernation.

Marsha regretted that she'd forgotten to make Wendy change into play clothes after school. Now her good socks and slacks were getting spattered with mud. Wendy giggled and squealed when her foot slid off the edge and dipped into the water. Her white sneakers were soon a comfortable shade of soggy tan.

"Wendy, come back! Stay on the path, please! Wendy, you're going to fall—again. Wendy, I told you! That's poison ivy, don't touch! Go wash your hands in the creek. Wendy, stop splashing!"

This is as bad as a shopping trip, thought Marsha. When they reached the highest part of the bank, she grabbed Wendy's hand. Here was real danger, a steep drop with only a few clumps of weeds and several saplings clinging to the wet, loose shale cliff to break a person's fall.

"What that?" Wendy yelled, her voice high and loud with excitement.

Oh, no. Marsha winced. She's found the rope swing.

Marsha tried to think of some clever and convincing explanation for a sturdy rope to be hanging invitingly next to a small ravine—some reason other than for swinging.

"Let me see!" Wendy struggled like a captured animal to free herself from Marsha's tightening grip. With one expert twist, she broke loose and scurried away.

"Wait!" Marsha screamed.

Wendy had, however, already reached the rope. Grabbing it with both hands, and giving a Tarzanesque yell, she leaped off the cliff into space.

Marsha stood frozen while her eyes followed the younger girl's progress out over the creek. Then she dropped the flyers and stumbled to the takeoff point, waited, and hoped.

Wendy's thin legs scrambled, her hair twirled out behind her, and her thin, wild scream pierced the stillness of the woods. She couldn't quite get a grip on the end of the rope with her legs and feet, but she somehow managed to hang on with her wiry hands.

As the rope swung back, Marsha reached for Wendy's legs.

"No!" Screaming and kicking viciously, she knocked Marsha's hands away.

"Wheee!" Wendy chortled as she sailed free. But her flight had been checked by Marsha's efforts to catch her, so the rope only swung partway out over the ravine.

The momentum was lost. The rope did not return to the ledge.

Wendy thrashed her legs and cried, "Marda! Marda! I gonna fall!"

With one glance at the long drop to the rocky creek, Marsha's whole body felt as unstable as the rain-soaked cliff. "Hang on! I'm coming!"

It seemed to take a long time for Marsha to backtrack along the path, slide down the bank, and stumble through the creek to a position under Wendy's feet.

"Okay, let go."

"No! No! No!" Higher and higher up the scale went Wendy's screams.

"Let go! I'll catch you."

"No!" Now Wendy was crying in earnest.

Marsha's neck hurt from staring up. "Hurry up, silly! Let go! I'm not going to stand here all day."

Without warning, Wendy dropped. Marsha caught her around the waist, staggered, and fell into the creek.

"I did it!" Wendy leaped up in triumph. She was like a tiny bantam rooster, crowing to the world.

"You? You did it?" sputtered Marsha. "Who caught you? Who saved you from smashing yourself on the rocks? Who has wet feet and wet jeans besides you? Me!"

"Again! I wanna do again!" Wendy started up the bank.

"Wait!" Marsha lunged and caught her by the hair.

"Ow! Let go!"

"No way! You sit right here on this rock. I have to go back up there and get my flyers. Don't you move."

Wendy's lower lip came out, and she glared up at her sister.

"And don't you dare have a screamy-meany! We have to

deliver those flyers, even though they're muddy, thanks to you. Then we're going straight home. Mom and Dad'll be home from work soon, and if you've been really good—I mean perfect—I'll take you over to Rosie's to see Lily's kittens."

"Lily? Not her kitties." Wendy tipped her head back and gave Marsha a superior stare. "They Princess' babies."

"Okay. Princess is their mommy. *Now sit!*"

Wendy sat while Marsha retrieved the smudged flyers.

The rest of the journey through the woods and up the long slope of the field to the first house was uneventful. Wendy's expression was dreamy, and she kept whispering, "Kitty, kitty. Kitty, kitty."

19

The house was still unoccupied although a sold sign had been recently planted in front of it. Spring weeds had sprouted around clods of exposed subsoil in the unseeded yard. There were no trees here or anywhere in the development, and the early afternoon sun reflected off the unused sidewalks—no chalked games of hopscotch, no muddy dog prints to break the newness. There was a desolate feeling about the place, and Marsha shivered despite the warmth of the air.

They went up to the front door, and Marsha jammed a rolled-up flyer behind the doorknob. She hoped whoever opened the door next would bother to read her message.

Following the new road up the hill, they stopped at each house on the right side. At the highest point, just where the road began its curve back downward, they found Dorey's house.

A new mailbox had been set at the end of the driveway.

Fresh earth was still lumped around the base of the post. The yard was covered with a thin layer of straw to protect the grass seed.

Out of the open garage, a short, shaggy dog appeared. He bounded toward the girls, barking hysterically.

"Snickers! Come back here." Dorey came running after him and caught him in her arms. She smiled and said, "Hi! It's about time you guys came to visit me!" The dog wriggled and took frantic licks at her face.

"We can't stay," said Marsha. "We have to get back home. We're just passing out flyers about the pony riding lessons I'm going to be giving this summer."

"Oh, yeah? I'll take one," said Dorey. "I have to baby-sit for my little brothers and sister sometimes. I'd love to get rid of Larry and Linda part of the time."

"I thought your brother's name was Bobby."

"It is. I have two brothers. Guess I like to pretend the other one doesn't exist. He's one of the Terrible Twosome. See? Here they come."

Dorey pointed at two small children who were pedaling Big Wheels out of the garage. They were the same size and were dressed identically in blue shorts and red T-shirts. Linda's hair was in a scraggly ponytail and was slightly darker than her brother's.

"Twins!" Wendy smiled broadly and stared.

"That's why we call them the Terrible Twosome. They're four now, but Mom—all of us—almost went crazy when they were real little."

Larry pedaled over to Wendy and gave her a toothy grin.

"Can you come inside?" Dorey asked Marsha. "I want to show you my room. My mom just made some cookies. Maybe she'll give us a pile of 'em."

"I guess I can come in for a minute." Marsha brushed some dried mud off her jeans.

"Cookie?" Wendy asked, tugging at Marsha's arm.

"Not right now. I'm going into Dorey's house for a second. You want to come in or stay out here and play?"

"Outside and play," said Wendy.

"Okay. I'll be right back. Don't go away."

Dorey's house still had the smell of fresh paint and new carpet. Marsha wiped her wet sneakers on the doormat and inspected them for mud before following Dorey into the spacious living room. Dorey plopped Snickers on a plush tan couch, then led the way to her bedroom.

It reminded Marsha of something pictured in a magazine. The bedspread and curtains matched, and the floor was covered with thick plum-colored carpet. On her bookshelves were neatly stacked games, and beneath her window stood a splendid Barbie dollhouse. There were enough stuffed toys to cover her bed and the top of her white bureau.

"Come on in the kitchen. Mom's trying out some new recipes with the microwave. She's feeling very domestic in her new kitchen." Dorey giggled. "I'll ask her for some cookies."

Dorey's mother didn't seem surprised or distressed at the appearance of her daughter's slightly dirty new friend. She gave each girl several warm chocolate chip cookies.

"Marsha has a pony, Mom. And she's going to be giving lessons to little kids this summer. You want to see her flyer?"

"What a clever idea!" her mother said when she saw the sheet. "How big is your pony?"

"Oh, he's part Shetland. So he's small. About this high." Marsha held out her hand, palm down, at the height of Butterscotch's back.

Suddenly, through the open kitchen window, came the sounds of an angry child's voice, and the crying began.

A screamy-meany, thought Marsha.

She was surprised to hear Dorey's mother say, "Sounds like Larry this time."

"I'll go check," Dorey offered.

Marsha trailed her new friend to the front door. There she took in the whole scene quickly. Larry was standing in the middle of the empty street, crying with his mouth wide open to create the maximum noise possible. Wendy was pedaling down the hill on his Big Wheel, which made a clattering racket almost as loud as his screams. Linda was riding her own vehicle around in circles, ignoring her brother. Coming up the hill from the opposite direction were Mike Adams and Dorey's brother Bobby.

"Wendy!" Marsha yelled. She pictured the sound waves she created being pummelled and destroyed by the ones already present. She hoped Wendy had sense enough to stop the Big Wheel when she reached the main road at the foot of the hill.

Larry's shrieks turned to words when he noticed a real audience. "That mean girl stole my Big Wheel!"

Marsha ran past the twins and after Wendy, but she didn't catch up until Wendy had turned around and was starting back up the hill.

"That's Larry's Big Wheel!" Marsha spat out the words between gulps for air.

"I know." Wendy kept pedaling.

"You shouldn't be riding it unless he said you could." Marsha jogged next to Wendy. She felt hot and angry and was uncomfortably aware of the other kids watching her. "Get off that stupid thing! You're way too big anyhow!"

Wendy shook her head. "No! No! No!" she chanted in time to each downward thrust on the pedals.

They finally made it back to the tear-streaked Larry. Wendy climbed off the Big Wheel and shoved it at him with her foot.

Frowning belligerently, she said, "Here, stupid boy. Retard!"

"Stop that, Wendy," Marsha whispered vehemently.

"You're the retard," Bobby told Wendy. "You're in that dummy class at school. I've seen you."

Marsha grabbed Wendy's hand.

"Bobby, shut up!" Dorey said.

"Nah, nah, nah," Bobby taunted. He was just warming up. "Wittle Wendy is a wetard!"

"Shut up!" Marsha didn't exactly shout the words, but she said them with such conviction and authority that Bobby stopped. Everyone stood perfectly still.

Marsha took a slow, deep breath. She sensed the space around her and was aware of the houses interrupting that space as they staggered down the hill on either side of the wide, black street. Somehow she felt strong, standing where she used to ride Butterscotch. Right here she would pull back on the reins and gaze down at the woods and off at the bluish, distant hills.

"Wendy is in that class, Bobby," she said carefully. "She is retarded. She acts younger than she looks. So, she grabs toys, and she calls people names . . ." Marsha looked at Bobby, but his eyes skittered away. "So . . . what's your excuse?"

No one said a single word, especially Bobby. Just then Linda began riding her Big Wheel in a circle around the group of children, and Larry pedaled after her.

The older children stood awkwardly. Marsha looked at Wendy and tried to smile, but her lips just twitched. She felt shaky, sure she'd cry if she said one more word.

"Come on, Mike. Let's get out of here." Bobby's voice was gruff. The two boys walked purposefully toward Mike's house. Suddenly Mike turned halfway around, waved, and winked.

Marsha lifted the hand that held Wendy's and managed a smile.

Dorey said, "Don't mind Bobby. He's just a ten-year-old hairball. Here, Wendy, have a cookie."

"Thanks," Wendy said quickly. Marsha squeezed her hand.

"We've got to go, Dorey."

"What about the rest of your flyers? I could take them around for you to the houses you haven't gotten to yet."

"Would you? Geez, thanks. I'll just keep a couple for kids at school."

"And Lily!" Wendy reminded her.

"Right."

Slowly and quietly the two girls walked home. All the way down the road, through the field, across the creek, and along the path, they held hands. It seemed to Marsha that neither of them wanted to let go.

20

The first few days of summer vacation were always strange, a mixture of freedom and boredom. Yet, this year was different. There was an uneasy tension between Marsha and her parents. She resisted thinking about the reason, unwilling to discuss it, refusing to say one word about her feelings toward Wendy. She wanted this summer to be like all the others—normal.

The afternoon of her birthday, Wendy ordered Marsha to stay out of the kitchen. "I helpin' Daddy make cake. Birthday cake for you!" she shouted gleefully.

"Oh, great!" Marsha groaned. "I can just imagine what it'll look like."

"Don't worry," David called from the kitchen. "It's going to be gorgeous. Wendy's picking the colors for the frosting, and I'm decorating it."

Marsha knew her father could draw well, but she wasn't at all sure he'd be able to manage the cake decorating tools.

"Why'd Mom go to town, anyhow? You guys decide I didn't have enough presents?"

"She's getting wrapping paper," David answered.

"Oh." Marsha leaned against the windowsill in the dining room. Memories of other birthdays floated with the scent of freshly cut grass. There was the year her dad made a gigantic clown, and all her friends played Pin the Nose on Bozo. On another birthday Aunt Laura sent a doll that could really eat. Of course, that meant it had to wear real diapers. Marsha fed it all the wrong foods, and pretty soon the insides of the doll were covered with mold. And then there was the Butterscotch birthday.

Marsha glanced around the dining room. It would've been fun to decorate with streamers and balloons. But she wasn't having a big party, just Rosie and Lily were coming for dinner and birthday cake. Maybe for Wendy's birthday they could have one of those neat kid parties with decorations and games and prizes. Maybe.

I wonder if I'll get my horse. The thought entered her mind before she had time to censor it. Really, though, Marsha told herself, I want to pick out my own horse. I'm not a six-year-old now.

She took another deep breath of the tantalizing air. From the kitchen came the murmur of her father and Wendy whispering conspiratorially. Marsha wondered what sort of concoction they were making.

The phone rang.

"Marsha! Can you get that? I'm busy," David called.

"Sure." She dashed upstairs and grabbed the receiver on the fourth ring.

It took Marsha a moment to place the caller's voice.

"Oh, Aunt Laura. Hi, how are you?"

"I'm just fine, Marsha. I'm calling to wish my favorite, one and only niece a very happy birthday."

"Thanks. You want to talk to Dad? He's right downstairs working in the kitchen."

"Well!" Aunt Laura laughed. "He certainly is a liberated male. Is he making something wonderful for your birthday dinner?"

"I guess so. He's decorating my cake now."

"Cake? Oh, yes. I suppose you must have those traditions. I hope it's carrot cake or something remotely nutritious."

"I sort of doubt it, Aunt Laura. I think it's just a regular cake with gobs of frosting."

Aunt Laura said quickly, "Don't eat too much and be sure to brush your teeth!"

"Okay. You want to talk to Dad? I'll run down and get him. Wendy's helping, so I'd better keep an eye on her while he's on the phone."

"No, it's your birthday, Marsha. I want to talk to you. Just the two of us."

Marsha plopped on the edge of her parents' bed and began to nibble her nails. She'd given up on her attempt to quit.

"I've wanted to have a chat with you for months," Laura continued. "I just haven't had the opportunity. I've been so busy at the shop. Merrilee, my partner, recently had a baby. She's been home on maternity leave, and I'm just beginning to catch my breath after a month on my own."

"Yeah, I bet," Marsha said, remembering too late that Aunt Laura disliked the word *yeah*.

"Well, now, how are you and that little retarded girl getting along?"

"Okay," Marsha answered as she spat a bit of nail out of her mouth.

"Marsha, I certainly hope this silly experiment of your parents hasn't been too difficult for you. I tried to talk them out of taking in such a child, but they wouldn't listen to reason. David used to take my advice. We used to be quite close, I think. He's wasting his life out there in the middle of nowhere, teaching farmers' children. But that's another whole issue . . ."

Marsha was frowning and squinting at the window as she listened. Here we go again, she thought. Why couldn't Aunt Laura realize that David loved his job? She wanted him to be something different—a wealthy lawyer or a famous artist, something he didn't want to be, or maybe something he couldn't be.

"Now, where was I?" Laura rattled on.

Where you always are—talking about the same old things, thought Marsha.

"I hope," went on Aunt Laura, "your parents have recovered their sanity and are going to send that girl back. They needn't feel any obligation to keep her."

"Her name's Wendy."

"Wendy? Oh, yes, I'd forgotten. How appropriate! A name from a frivolous fairy tale about children who refuse to grow up."

"Wendy's okay," Marsha said quickly. Talking to Aunt Laura and the bright afternoon sun's glare on the window were making her head hurt.

"Oh, Darling! You don't have to say that. I know how you must feel with the other children teasing you, people staring. I honestly think those retarded children would be better off living in special institutions."

"What?" Marsha was beginning to feel slightly nauseated. Maybe I'm just hungry, she thought.

"Never mind, Darling. I really wanted to talk about something else. I have a simply grand idea for you and me! It's my birthday present to you. I'm taking my vacation as soon as Merrilee comes back to work and I'd like you to spend it in New York with me. I'll show you off to my friends. We'll go see a Broadway play. Doesn't that sound like fun?"

Marsha swallowed. The hum of the electric mixer was barely audible from the kitchen.

"Well, what do you think?" persisted Aunt Laura.

"Thanks. But I don't really know . . ."

"Don't worry. I'll take care of your parents. I'll convince them that you must get away from what's her name . . . Wendy."

"Honest, Aunt Laura. Wendy's fine!"

"Marsha, you don't need to lie to me. I understand."

"No, you don't!" Marsha's heart began to hammer hard. "You don't understand me, or Wendy, or even David. And you're wrong about Wendy in _Peter Pan,_ too. She does grow up. She comes back from Neverland. Don't you remember?"

Laura gave a high, tense laugh. "No, I must admit, I don't recall the story very well. Your father has always been the reader in the family. I hope I haven't hurt your feelings, Marsha. I'm only trying to help you. I know that sometimes parents don't listen to or understand their children. But if you don't want to come to New York, just say so. I can always send you a check to buy clothes or something special."

"Thanks, Aunt Laura. I really don't think I want to come. I mean, there's so much going on here. I'm going to be giving riding lessons on my pony. And some of my friends and I are going to be going to the swimming pool in town a lot."

The rest of the conversation was polite but stilted.

Unbelievable! Marsha thought after she had said, "Good-bye," and hung up. I stood up to Aunt Laura!

When her mother arrived home, Marsha was banished to her room so the last minute wrapping could be accomplished. She sat on her top bunk, staring down at her model horse shelf. J.J. came in, leaped up, and climbed into her lap. He purred softly, rubbing against her stomach. She pulled him close and kissed him on the head.

"Marsha! Come on down. We're finished wrapping, and here come Rosie and Lily!" Kate called up.

For dinner there was spaghetti with her mother's homemade sauce and heaps of grated cheddar cheese on top. Wendy had a chopped-up hot dog mixed into her sauce.

"Look, Lily!" Wendy yelled across the table. She held up her fork with five chunks of hot dog expertly speared on several prongs. Lily laughed appreciatively, and Wendy bounced up and down in her chair.

This was Wendy's first celebration of any kind in the O'Dells' home. Marsha wondered what Christmas would be like with Wendy. Maybe she'd climb the Christmas tree or eat the decorations.

When dinner was over, Wendy helped clear the table and only dropped one plate. It didn't break, which Marsha decided was a good sign.

"Are you getting a horse?" Rosie whispered into Marsha's ear.

She shook her head and said aloud, "No. I'm going to buy one for myself."

"Listen to our little girl," David said with a grin. "I guess twelve is even more grown-up than I realized."

"Where're the presents?" asked Lily.

"Whee! Presents! Presents! Presents!" chanted Wendy.

"Let's have Marsha open them now, and we'll have cake and ice cream last," Kate suggested.

Wendy and Lily ran to the hall closet and dragged out a large paper bag.

"First open the ones you got in the mail from relatives," Rosie suggested.

"There is one that arrived last week," said David. "It's from Grandma O'Dell in California."

Marsha unwrapped it quickly and was surprised to find a camera, complete with film and flash. Usually her grandmother sent baby dolls or dresses that were too small. Evidently even Grandma realized that Marsha was growing up.

Rosie looked at the camera and began to laugh. "I can't believe it! Wait'll you see my present."

"It's from both of us," piped up Lily.

The package looked too big for a diary even though it felt like one. When Marsha ripped apart the bright wrapping paper, there was a blue photo album with a picture of a white horse on the cover.

"Honest," Rosie said. "I didn't know about the camera. I just thought since we're going into junior high, and we'll be doing lots of stuff, it'd be neat, you know, to have some place to keep pictures. And when I saw the horse on that album, I had to get it for you."

"Thanks! It's absolutely perfect!" exclaimed Marsha.

Wendy was busy attempting to unwrap two of the remaining presents, so Marsha decided to help her.

There were a new blouse, a pair of jeans, and some socks. One unopened package was very lumpy and awkward. Marsha could tell from the quantity of extra long and twisted tape that Wendy had wrapped it.

After struggling through the layers of paper and tape, Marsha stared at the present and then looked up into her parents' smiling faces.

"We thought because you're going to be paying for your own horse, the least we could do was buy you a bridle," her mother said.

"Come on! Time for cake! Cake time!" Wendy yelled, interrupting Marsha's thanks. "I wanna carry!"

"Okay, Honey. But let me put your hair back in a ponytail so it won't catch fire. Lots of candles on that cake," Kate said.

"Now, we have a special event coming up," announced David. "Not only is Wendy carrying this phenomenal cake, but she's also going to sing 'Happy Birthday' all by herself. It's her present to Marsha."

David turned off the lights. From the kitchen came a wavering glow which moved toward the dining room.

As Wendy reached the table, her face above the flickering candles shown in the soft light. She never took her eyes off the cake, but her slightly off-key voice reached out to Marsha.

"Happy birthday to you. Happy birthday to you. Happy birthday, dear *Marsha* . . ." The rest of the song came out in a rush as she set the cake down in front of Marsha.

"Blow 'em out! Come on, Marsha! Make wish," Wendy begged.

Marsha blew, and all the candles winked out just before her father turned the lights back on.

"Oh, what a great cake! Dad, the horse is fantastic," said Marsha.

There was a blue and red horse on the rectangular cake. Surrounding the horse were squiggles of orange and green. At each corner, a pink flower blossomed, and the candles were striped yellow and white.

"Gee, Mr. O'Dell," Lily said sincerely, "I didn't know you were a cake decorator."

"Marsha! Marsha! I picked colors!" Wendy hopped on one foot then the other.

"I know. I can tell. Thank you, Wendy."

"What'd you wish for?" asked Lily.

"Oh, no," Rosie said. "She can't tell. It's a secret. If she tells, it won't come true!"

"It's okay. I wished for something I *know* will come true," said Marsha.

"What? That you'll get a horse?" Lily asked.

"No!" Marsha looked up and met her mother's eyes. "I wished for a sister who can say my name."

"I can say name!" Wendy shrieked. "I worked and worked. Mommy helped. So I can say for birthday. *Happy birthday, Marsha!*"

21

July
This isn't a diary anymore, I've decided. I won't be writing Dear Diary at the top. That was like writing to an imaginary friend . . . sort of babyish, I think. I'm going to call this a journal, even though there are only a few pages left. I'll have to get something else to write in.

I'm really teaching riding! I have five little kids who come for lessons twice a week. Maybe taking care of Wendy has helped me to know how to get along better with kids younger than me. I mean, who could be worse than Wendy?

I'm saving all the money I earn from the lessons

toward buying my horse. Every day I read the ads in the paper. "Chestnut mare, seven years, well trained" or "Palomino gelding, excellent trail horse." But I keep looking for a black stallion—or maybe a white one like Flicka's colt.

Today we went to court, and now Wendy is my real sister forever. She's not so bad, I guess. She plays with Rosie's sisters a lot, especially Lily.

Wendy has picked out her kitten from the litter in Rosie's barn. It's tiger striped, real cute. She calls him Tiger. What else? I've asked Kate and David if she can have the kitten for her birthday, and they said yes.

I haven't told J.J. yet. Maybe he'll get back to being my cat once the new kitten moves in.

Ever since my birthday, Wendy's been saying my name right most of the time. Funny. I sort of miss being Marda. I don't think she'll ever ride Butterscotch. And I know I can't make her.

Aunt Laura decided to vacation in Europe since I didn't visit her this summer. She even sent Wendy and me postcards from some zoo over there. I gave mine to Wendy because it has a picture of a tiger on it. Wendy likes her card, too, even though it has a picture of an elephant. I think she likes it because she can read some of what Aunt Laura wrote on it.

That reminds me. We went out to eat for lunch to celebrate after the adoption was made official. Mom showed Wendy the menu, and Wendy could read what she wanted. Guess what she ordered. A hot dog. Actually, three. Surprise!

Sheila Kelly Welch was born in Pennsylvania and became interested in writing and drawing while in elementary school. She majored in Fine Arts at Temple University in Philadelphia. After receiving her Masters in Education, she taught developmentally delayed children in Pennsylvania and in Minnesota.

The author has been writing children's short stories for several years. Her work has been published or accepted by *Cricket, The Friend, Children's Playmate,* and *Highlights for Children.* Currently she is working on a collection of horse stories for young readers.

She and her husband, Eric, have seven children, six of whom joined the family through adoption. They share their country home near Forreston, Illinois with six horses, five dogs, and seven cats.